Roy Blakeley: His Story

Percy Keese Fitzhugh

Roy Blakeley: His Story

CHAPTER I. TROUBLES OF MY OWN – THE BIG CONCLAVE

Well, here I am at last, ready to tell you the adventures of our young lives. Right away I have trouble with Pee-wee Harris. He's about as easy to keep down as a balloon full of gas. We call him the young dirigible because he's always going up in the air. Even at the start he must stick in his chapter heading about a conclave.

Hanged if I know what a conclave is. It's some kind of a meeting I guess. He said it was something like a peace conference, but believe me, the meeting I'm going to tell you about wasn't much like a peace conference. I told him I'd use my own heading and his too, just to keep him quiet. I think he's got his pockets stuffed full of chapter headings and that he'll be shooting them at me all the way through – like a machine – gun.

I guess I might as well tell you about Pee-wee before I tell you about the conclave or whatever you call it He's Doctor Harris's son and he's a member of the Raven Patrol. He's a member in good standing, only he doesn't stand very high. Honest, you can hardly see him without a magnifying glass. But for voice – good night!

He sings in the Methodist Church choir and they say he can throw his voice anywhere. I wish he'd throw it in the ash barrel, I know that. He always wears his belt-axe to troop meetings, in case the Germans should invade Bridgeboro, I suppose. He's the troop mascot and if you walk around him three times and ruffle up his beautiful curly hair, you can change your luck.

Well, now I'll tell you about the meeting. We had a big special meeting to decide about two things, and believe me, those two things had momentous consequences. Momentous – that's a good word, hey?

One thing, we wanted to decide about our campaign for collecting books for soldiers, and another thing, we wanted to decide how we could all go up to Temple Camp in our cabin launch, the Good Turn.

This large arid what—do—you—call—it launch—I mean commodious launch—is a dandy boat, except for one thing—the bow is too near the stern. If we were sardines instead of boy scouts, it would be all right, but you see there's twenty-four of us altogether, not counting Captain Kidd, our mascot—he's a parrot.

So I got up and said, "How are we going to crowd twenty—four growing boys and a parrot into a twenty foot launch?"

"It can't be did," Doc Carson shouted. "Then some of us will have to hike it on our dear little feet," I said.

"Or else we'll have to get a barge or something or other and tow it," Artie Van Arlen said.

"What, with a three horse-power engine?" somebody else shouted.

"You can bet I won't be one of the ones to hike it," Pee-wee yelled; "I'll dope out some scheme or other."

And believe me, he did.

Well, after we'd been talking about an hour or so on how we'd manage it, Mr. Ellsworth, our scoutmaster, up and said there was plenty of time for that as long as we were not going to camp for a couple of weeks anyway, and that we'd better begin thinking of how we were going to start about collecting books for soldiers.

All the while I had something very important to or say, and I was kind of trembling, as you might say, "for I thought maybe Mr. Ellsworth wouldn't like the idea. Anyway I got up and began:

"The author that wrote all about 'Tom Slade's adventures in the World War'," I said, "told me it would be a good idea for one to write up our troop's adventures and he'd help me to get them published."

Then up jumped Pee-wee Harris like a jack—in—the—box.

"What are you talking about?" he shouted; "don't you know you have to have a command of language to write books? You're crazy!"

3

"I should worry about a command of language," I told him. "Haven't I got command of the Silver Fox Patrol? Anybody who can command the Silver Fox Patrol ought to be able to command a few languages and things. I could command a whole regiment even," I kept up, for I saw that Pee-wee was getting worked up, as usual, and all the fellows were laughing, even Mr. Ellsworth.

"If you could command a division," Westy Martin said, in that sober way of his, "you ought to be able to command English all right."

"I can command any kind of a division," I shouted, all the while winking at Westy, "I can command a long division or a short division or a multiplication or a subtraction or a plain addition."

"What are you talking about?" Pee-wee yelled.

"You're crazy!"

"I can command anything except Pee-wee Harris's temper," I said.

Well, you ought to have seen Pee-wee. Even Mr. Ellsworth had to laugh.

"How can a fellow your age write books?" he fairly screamed. "You have to have sunsets and twilights and gurgling brooks and—"

"You leave the gurgling brooks to me," I said; "I'll make them gurgle all right. There's going to be plenty of action in these books. And Pee-wee Harris is going to be the village cut-up." "Are you going to have girls?" he shouted.

"Sure I'm going to have girls—gold haired girls—all kinds—take your pick."

"Good night!" Pee-wee shouted, "I see your finish."

Well, pretty soon everybody was shouting at the same time and Pee-wee was dancing around, saying we were all crazy. Most of the Raven Patrol were with him and they ought to be called the Raving Patrol, believe me. Then Mr. Ellsworth held up his hand in that quiet way he has. "This sounds like the Western Front or a Bolshevik meeting," he said, "and I'm afraid our young Raven, Mr. Pee-wee Harris, will presently explode and that would be an unpleasant episode for any book."

"Good night!" I said. "Don't want any of my books to end with an explosion."

Then he said how it would be a good idea for me to write up our adventures and how he'd help me whenever I got stuck and how he guessed the author of Tom Slade would put in fancy touches for me, because he lives in our town and he's a whole lot interested in our troop. He said that breezes and distant views and twilights and things aren't so hard when you get used to them and even storms and hurricanes are easy if you only know how. He said girls aren't so easy to manage though.

"I'll help you out with the girls," Pee-wee said; "I know all about girls. And I'll help you with the names of the chapters, too."

"All right," Mr. Ellsworth said, "I think Pee-wee will prove a valuable collaborator."

"A which?" Pee-wee said, kind of frightened.

So then we all laughed and Mr. Ellsworth said it was getting late and we'd better settle about collecting books for the soldiers.

We decided that after we got to camp I'd begin writing up our adventures on the trip, but we couldn't decide how we'd all go in our boat, and that was the thing that troubled us a lot, because the fellows in our troop always hang together and we didn't like the idea of being separated.

Well, I guess that's all there is to tell you about the meeting, and in the next chapter I'm going to tell you all about how we collected the books for the fellows in camp, and how the mystery about the boat was solved. Those are Pee-wee's words about the mystery of the boat. I can't see that there was any mystery about it, but there was another kind of a mystery, believe me, and that kid was the cause of it. I guess maybe you'll like the next chapter better than this one.

So long.

CHAPTER II. SWATTING THE SPY

Now I'm going to tell you about how we collected books for soldiers and especially about Pee-wee's big stunt.

The next morning we started out and by night we had over five hundred books. Mr. Ellsworth said they were mostly light literature, but if he had only had to carry fifty of them on his shoulder like I did, he'd have thought they were pretty heavy literature, believe me.

This is the way we fixed it. The Raving Patrol, (that's Pee-wee's patrol, you know) used Doctor Harris's five-passenger Fraud car. It didn't go very good and Pumpkin Odell (Raven) said he guessed it was because the wheels were tired—that's a joke. They held up all the houses in Little Valley. That's about sumpty—seven miles or so from Bridgeboro. They've got two stores there and a sign that says "Welcome to Automobilists" and how they'll be arrested if they don't obey the speed laws. Welcome to jail— good night!

The Elk Patrol (that's our new patrol, you know) went over to East Bridgeboro with Pinky Dawson's express wagon (one horse power) and some horse—I wish you could see him. The Elks were a pretty lively bunch, I'll say that, and they cleaned out all the private libraries in East Bridgeboro. They even got cook-books and arithmetics and books about geometry—pity the poor soldiers.

The Silver Fox Patrol took care of Bridgeboro. That's the best patrol of the whole three. I'm leader of the Silver Foxes. The Ravens call us the Silver-plated Foxes, but that's because we can them the Raving Patrol and the reason we call them the Raving Patrol is on account of Pee-wee.

Let's see, where was I? Oh yes, the Silver Foxes took care of Bridgeboro. Brick Warner (He's red-headed) has a Complex car or a Simplex, or whatever you call it—I should worry. I mean his father has it. He's got a dandy father; he gave Brick five dollars so that we could have a blow—out at lunch time. Oh, boy, we had two blow—outs and a puncture.

We got over two hundred books that day — light literature, dark literature, all colors. I could tell you a lot of things that happened that day, because we did a lot of good turns, and one bad turn, when we grazed a telegraph pole. What cared we? But you'll care more about hearing of Pee-wee and the raving Ravens and how they made out. ...

Anyway, I guess I might as well tell you now about the scouts in my patrol. Don't ever borrow trouble, but get to be a patrol leader, and you'll have troubles of your own. Then you can pick out the one you want and I'll drown the rest. After that I'll tell you about the grand drive in Little Valley.

First in the Silver Fox Patrol comes Roy Blakeley — that's me. I'm patrol leader and I've got eleven merit badges. I've got two sisters too. One of them is crazy about the movies.

I've got seven scouts to look after and Captain Kidd, the parrot — he's our mascot. Our patrol color is green and he's green with a yellow neck. He's got one merit badge-for music. Good night! Then comes Westy Martin, and Dorry Benton and Huntley Manners and Sleuth Seabury, because he's a good detective, and Will Dawson and Brick Warner and Slick Warner and that's all.

Now I'll tell you about the raving Ravens. Of course, I can't tell you all that happened in Little Valley that day, because I wasn't there. Doc Carson said they had trouble with the motor and Pee-wee. He said that Pee-wee kept running wild an day. But anyway they brought back a lot of books with them, I'll say that much.

Well, when the day's drive was over, we all took our books to the troop room and piled them up on the table, and waited for Mr. Ellsworth to come. He usually comes home from the city on the Woolworth Special. We call it the Woolworth Special because it gets to Bridgeboro at five ten. Along about six o'clock he showed up, and we began sorting out the books. The biggest pile was brought in by the Ravens, and when he noticed a pile of about twenty or thirty books tied with a brown cord, he asked where those came from. Then up jumped Pee-wee, very excited, and said: "I'll tell you about those."

"Do tell," said Elmer Sawyer, winking at me.

"Good night! Pee-wee's got the floor," shouted Westy.

"Floor!" shouted Dorry Benton. "He's got the walls and the ceiling and the mantelpiece and everything."

"Will you pay a little attention?" Pee-wee screamed.

"We're paying as little as possible," I told him.

"You're the worst of the lot," he yelled; "that pile of books, the ones with the brown cord, were given to us by a kindly old gentleman; he—.

"A which?" Doc Carson said.

"Don't you know a kindly old gentleman when you see one?" Pee-wee fairly screamed.

"Let's see one," Artie shouted.

And that's the way it went on till Mr. Ellsworth came to Pee-wee's rescue like he always does. He said we should let Pee-wee have the chair.

"Here's a couple of chairs for him," we shouted.

"He can have the table too, if he wants it," I said; anything to keep him quiet.

"I don't want to be quiet," Pee-wee screamed.

Good night, that was some meeting. Well, pretty soon Mr. Ellsworth got us all throttled down and Pee-wee started to tell us about his visit to the kindly old gentleman. It seemed that was one of the houses that Pee-wee called at alone and the kindly old gentleman fell for him like grown up people mostly do. I don't know what it is but everybody seems to like Pee-wee. You know just because you jolly a fellow, it's not a sign you don't like him. Pee-wee is one bully little scout, I'll say that much.

"Do you want to hear about it?" he said.

8

"Proceed with your narrative," I told him; "begin at the beginning, go on till you come to the end, then stop."

"Be sure to stop," Westy said.

Well, then Pee-wee went on to tell us about the kindly old gentleman. He lived in a big white house, he said, with grounds around it and a big flag pole on the lawn, with a flag flying from it. He said that the old gentleman didn't talk very good English and he thought maybe he was a German or French or something or other. He guessed maybe he was a professor or something like that. Anyway, he took Pee-wee through his library, picking out the books he didn't want, till be had given him about twenty or thirty. Then they tied them up in a brown cord and Pee-wee took them out to the Fraud car.

Well that's about all there was to it, and I guess nothing more would have happened, if I hadn't untied the cord and picked up the book that lay on top. It was a book about German history, princes and all that stuff, and I guess it wouldn't interest soldiers much. Just as I was running through it, I happened to notice a piece of paper between the leaves, which I guess the old gentleman put there for a book-mark. As soon as I picked it up and read it, I said, "Good night! Look at this," and I handed it to Mr. Ellsworth.

It said something about getting information to Hindenburg, and about how a certain German spy was in one of the American camps in France.

Mr. Ellsworth read it through two or three times, and then said, "Boys, this looks like a very serious matter. You said the old gentleman spoke broken English, Walter?"

That's the name he always called Pee-wee.

"Cracky," I said, "Pee-wee's kindly old gentleman is a German spy."

"Sure he is," said Westy Martin, "and he's only flying the American flag for a bluff, he's a deep dyed villain."

"He can't be dyed very deep," said Doc Carson, in that sober way of his; "because we haven't any German dyes to dye him with."

I was just going to say something to kid Pee-wee along, when I noticed that Mr. Ellsworth was very serious, and Pee-wee was staring like a ghost.

"Boys," Mr. Ellsworth said, "I have no idea of the full meaning of this paper." Then he said how maybe in collecting books we had caught a spy in our net. He said that he was going to take the paper anyway and show it to the Federal Commissioner, down in the Post Office Building.

"If he's a spy, we'll swat him all right," I said.

"We'll more than swat him," Mr. Ellsworth said, and I could see by the look in his eye that he meant business.

CHAPTER III. SWATTING THE SPY—CONTINUED

We didn't swat him in that chapter because I had to go to supper, but we'll surely swat him in this one. Positively guaranteed.

Pee-wee was proud that he made such a hit with the old gentleman and especially because he got so many books from him. But when he realized that the paper I found in one of the books had something to do with spying, it was all Mr. Ellsworth could do to keep him quiet. He told us all not to say anything, because maybe, the old man might find out that he was going to be nabbed and go away. I guess Pee-wee felt pretty important. Anyway I know he was frightened, because all the next morning he kept asking me if he'd have to go to court and things like that.

"The only court you'll go to, is the tennis court," I told him; so we made up a set with my two sisters, Ruth and Marjorie, and the girls beat us three games. While we were playing, along came Mr Ellsworth and Commissioner Terry with two strange men, and I could see Pee-wee was very nervous. They sent the girls away and then began to ask Pee-wee questions. I could see that they thought the discovery we made was pretty serious.

"Are you the boy that found the paper in the book?" they asked me. Then they wanted to know what kind of a book it was, and I told them it was a book about German history and they screwed up their faces and looked very suspicious.

"You say that the man spoke broken English?" one of them asked Pee-wee.

Pee-wee was kind of nervous, I could see. "It—it—well it wasn't exactly broken," he said.

"Just a little bent," I said, and oh, you ought to have seen the frown Mr. Ellsworth gave me.

"It was kind of—just a little—" Pee-wee began.

"We understand," one of the men said. Then the other one spoke to us. He said, "Boys, we want you to go over with us and we want this youngster to identify the man. You needn't be afraid, Uncle Sam is with you."

But, cracky, I didn't like it and I guess Pee-wee didn't either. I've read stories about boys that had men arrested and all that, and I always thought I'd like to be one of those regular heroes. But when it came to really doing it, I knew then that I didn't like to help arrest anybody, and I bet most real fellows feel the same way. I felt funny, kind of. That's why I have no use for young detectives in stories, because I know you've got to be a grown-up man to feel that way and do things like that.

They had an automobile right near the tennis courts and we all got in and Pee-wee and I sat in back with our scoutmaster. Cracky, I was glad our scoutmaster was along, that's one sure thing. Pretty soon we got to Little Valley and Pee-wee pointed out the big white house with the lawn and the flag flying there. Jiminy, but it looked good and I wished we were up at Temple Camp, raising our colors near the boat landing.

While we were going up the gravel path; the old gentleman came out on his porch and looked at us and I felt kind of ashamed and I could see Pee-wee did too. But, cracky, I've got no use for spies, that's one sure thing. Pee-wee and I kind of hung behind and I guess he felt funny, sort of, when the old gentleman waved his hand to him, as if they were old friends.

I can't remember all they said but the two men who I knew were detectives showed the old gentleman the paper and asked him what it meant. First he seemed kind of flustered and angry and I know Pee-wee's heart was thumping-anyway it would have been thumping, except that it was up in his throat.

Then the men said that they'd have to search the house to see if there was a wireless and then the old gentleman got angry; then all of a sudden he sat down in one of the wicker chairs on the porch and began to laugh and laugh and laugh. Then he looked at Pee-wee and said, "I suppose this is the young gentleman who succeeded in trapping me. I must take off my hat to the Boy Scouts," and he smiled with an awful pleasant kind of a smile and held out his hand to Pee-wee.

Well, you should have seen Pee-wee. It was as good as a three-ringed circus. He stood there as if he was posing for animal crackers. And even the detectives looked kind of puzzled, but all the while suspicious.

"Are you the spy-catcher?" the old gentleman said to Pee-wee, but Pee-wee looked all flabbergasted and only shifted from one foot to the other.

"I hope you don't mean to kill me with that belt. axe?" the old gentleman asked. But Pee-wee just couldn't speak.

"He must be a telephone girl—'he doesn't answer," I blurted out, and even the detectives had to laugh.

"Gentlemen, if you will step inside, I'll make full confession and then give myself up," the old man said; "for I see there is no use in trying to escape the Boy Scouts. It was I who wrote that treasonable memorandum and I may as well tell you that I have a wireless. I will give you my whole history. I see that my young friend here is a most capable secret service agent."

"We're only small boys—we belong to the infantry," I said, for I just couldn't help blurting it out.

Well, we all went inside and I could see that the Commissioner and the detectives kept very near the old gentleman as if they didn't have much use for his laughing and his pleasant talk. I guess maybe they were used to that kind of thing, and he couldn't fool them.

When we got into his library I saw books all around on the shelves, hundreds of them I guess, and the desk was covered with papers and there was a picture of Mark Twain with "Best regards to Mr. Donnelle," written on it. Gee whit taker, I thought when I looked around; maybe Mr. Donnelle is a deep-dyed spy all right, but he's sure a high-brow.

"You'd have to take an elevator to get up to him," I whispered to Pee-wee.

"Shhh," Pee-wee said, "maybe he isn't dyed so very deep—there's different shades of dyes."

"Maybe he's only dyed a light gray or a pale blue," I said.

Then Mr. Donnelle got out a big fat red book that said on it "Who's Who in America" and, jiminy, I'm glad I never had to study it, because it had about a million pages. I hate biography anyway—biography and arithmetic. Then he turned to a certain page.

"Now, gentlemen," he said, "if you will just read this I will then consent to go with you," and he smiled all over his face.

The four men leaned over and began reading, but Pee-wee and I didn't because they didn't ask us and Boy Scouts don't butt in.

"I bet it tells all about German spies and everything, and now he's going to make a full confession," Pee-wee said; "maybe our names will be in the New York papers, hey?"

"They'll be more likely to be in the fly-paper," I said; "there's something funny about this."

"I bet he was going to blow up some ships," Pee-wee said.

"I bet he'll blow us up in a minute," I told him; because I could see that he was saying something to the men while they all looked at the book, and that the whole four of them were laughing—especially Mr. Ellsworth.

"It was the elder boy who discovered it," I heard him say, smiling all the while.

"Good night!" I said to Pee-wee, "I thought we had a German in custody, but instead of that. We're in Dutch!"

"Will they send us to jail?" he whispered.

"I think we'll get about ten merit badges for this—not," I said; "he's no spy."

Well, the men didn't pay much attention to us, only strolled over to one side of the room and began chatting together, and Mr. Donnelle got a box of cigars and they each took one.

"I wouldn't smoke one of those cigars," Pee-wee said, "they might be bombs. The Germans are pretty tricky—safety first."

Then Mr. Ellsworth came over to us, smiling all over his face. "Well, boys," he said, "I'm glad to say that our spy quest has gone up in smoke. Mr. Donnelle is one of the best known authors of America. He is writing a story of the war and our dark memorandum is just a little literary note of his about a spy among the American forces. I think we shall find it a most interesting story when it is finished. It is full of German intrigue and you will be glad to know that the imaginary spy is caught and court-martialled. You have done a fine thing by your discovery, for Mr. Donnelle has become greatly interested in the Scouts, and especially in our young scout author." Then he gave me a funny look. "So you see our dark memorandum was not so dark after all."

"G—o—o—d night!" I said; "it was a kind of a pale white."

"And I dare say," Mr. Ellsworth said, all the while slapping me on the shoulder, "that our deep-dyed villain is going to prove a very good friend."

"Even if you're deep-dyed," said Pee-wee, "sometimes the colors will run and you won't be so deep-dyed after all. My sister had a skirt and she dyed it a deep—"

Honest, that kid is a scream.

CHAPTER IV. THE PLOT GROWS THINNER — OR ELSE THICKER

Pee-wee says it grows thicker and I say it grows thinner, so I put it both ways. I told him things would begin to stir up in this chapter and he said a thing always gets thicker when you stir it. I should worry.

"Suppose we should go boating or something like that where there's a lot of water," I told him; "that would thin it some if you added water wouldn't it?"

"You're crazy," he shouted.

Westy Martin wanted to name it The Deep Dyed Villain — so you can call it that if you want to — I don't care.

Now I'll start off. You remember about Mr. Donnelle saying that he had a wireless. Well, pretty soon after what I've been telling you about, the men went away and they were all laughing and good natured about it. I heard one of them say that the Boy Scouts were a wide — awake lot. Believe me, they wouldn't say that if they saw us sleeping after a day's hike at Temple Camp. If you heard Vic Norris snore, you'd think it was the West Front in France.

Well anyway, Mr. Donnelle wanted Pee-wee and me to stay at his house a little while, because he said he was kind of interested in us. He would listen to Pee-wee very sober like and then begin to laugh. And whenever Pee-wee tried to explain, it only made him laugh more.

"Anyway, I could see you weren't a very bad kind of a spy," Pee-wee said. Jiminetty, I had to laugh.

Well, Mr. Donnelle asked us all about the Scouts and we told him all about them — Pee-wee mostly did that. He's a scout propagander let— that's a small sized propagandist. We told him, how we didn't know how we are going to manage to get up to Temple Camp in our launch, because it would only hold about seven or eight boys and we had twenty-four, not counting Captain Kidd, the parrot.

"Well, now I have a little scheme," he said, smiling all the while, "and perhaps we can hit some sort of a plan. If I can only get you boys out of the way, away up at camp, I'll be able to carry on my German propaganda work." Then he winked at me and I knew he was kidding Pee-wee. Well, believe me, we hit a plan all right; we more than hit it, we gave it a knockout blow. All the while we were talking, he was taking us across the lawn till pretty soon we came to a little patch of woods and as soon as I got a whiff of those trees, good night, I felt as if I was up at Temple Camp already. That's a funny thing about trees — you get to know them and like them sort of.

Then pretty soon we came to a creek that ran through the woods and I could see it was deep and all shaded by the trees. Oh, jiminy, it was fine. And you could hear it ripple too, just like the water of Black Lake up near Temple Camp. If I was a grown-up author I could write some dandy stuff about it, because it was all dark and spooky as you might say, and you could see the trees reflected in it and casting their something or other — you know what I mean.

"Can you follow a trail?", Mr. Donnelle asked us.

"Trails are our middle names;" I told him, "and I can follow one — "

"Whitherso'er — " Pee-wee began.

"Whither so which?" I said. Because he was trying to talk high brow just because he knew Mr. Donnelle was an author.

So he led us along a trail that ran along the shore all in and out through trees, and he said it was all his property. Pretty soon I could see part of a house through the trees and I thought I'd like to live there, it was so lonely.

"You mean secluded," Pee-wee said. Mr. Donnelle smiled and I told him Pee-wee was a young dictionary — pocket size.

Pretty soon we reached the house and, good night, it wasn't any house at all; it was a house boat. And I could see the fixtures for a wireless on it, only the wires had been taken down.

Then Mr. Donnelle said, "Boys," he said, "this is my old workshop and I have spent many happy hours in it. But I don't use it any more and if you boys think you could all pile into it, why you are welcome to it for the summer. It has no power, but perhaps you could tow it behind your launch. Anyway you may charter it for the large sum of nothing at all, as a reward for foiling a spy."

"I—I kind of knew you were not a spy all the time," said Pee-wee.

Well, I was so flabbergasted that I just couldn't speak and even Pee-wee was struck dumb. We just gaped like a couple of idiots, and after a while I said, "Cracky, it's too good to be true."

"So you see what comes from collecting books for soldiers and for keeping your eyes open," Mr. Donnelle said; "you have caught a bigger fish than you thought. N ow suppose I show you through the inside."

Now here is the place where the plot begins to get thicker and, believe me, in four or five chapters it will be as thick as mud. We were just coming up to the house-boat to go aboard it, when suddenly the door flew open and a fellow scampered across the deck and ran away.

I could see that he had pretty shabby clothes and a peaked cap and I guess he was startled to hear us coming. In just a few seconds he was gone in the woods and we all stood gaping there while the boat bobbed up and down, on account of him jumping from it. But I got a squint at his face all right, and I noticed the color of his cap and how he ran, and I'm mighty glad I did, because that fellow was going to come into our young lives again and cause us a lot of trouble, you can bet.

Mr. Donnelle said he was probably just a tramp that had been sleeping in the boat and he didn't seem to mind much, only he said it would be better to keep the door locked.

"Maybe he might have been a—" Pee-wee began.

"No siree," I said. "We've had enough of deep-dyed villains for one day, if that's what you were going to say."

"Maybe we'd better track him," said Pee-wee, very serious.

"Nix on the tracking," I said, "I've retired from the 'detective business, and now I'm going to be cook on a house-boat."

"We'll have a good anchor anyway if you make biscuits," Pee-wee said.

"They'll weigh more than you do anyway," I fired back.

And Mr. Donnelle began to laugh.

Well, we didn't bother our heads any more about the tramp, but I could see that Pee-wee would have been happier if we'd have thought it was the Kaiser or Villa, instead of just a plain ordinary tramp, looking for a place to sleep. But oh, crinkums, you'll be surprised when you hear all about that fellow and who he was and I suppose you'd like me to tell you now, wouldn't you? But I won't.

I've got to go to camp meeting now, so goodbye, see you later —

CHAPTER V. LOST

Now I'm going to write until my sister begins playing the piano. Music and literature don't mix—believe me. There are two cruises in this book—a big one and a little one. You can take your pick. The little one is full of mud and the big one is full of pep. Anyway you get your money's worth, that's one sure thing.

This chapter is about the little cruise. But first I have to tell you about the house-boat, because it turned out to be our home sweet home for a couple of weeks. It didn't only turn out, but it turned in and it turned sideways and every which way. But I'm not going to knock it. It got knocks enough going through the creek and up Bridgeboro River. It knocked into two bridges, and goodness knows what all. But what cared we, yo ho? We cared not—I mean naught.

First Mr. Donnelle showed us through it and it was dandy, only in very poor shape. It's shape was square. But I wouldn't laugh at it because we had a lot of fun on it. Inside it had two rooms and a little kitchen and the roof had a railing around it and there was lots of room there. There was lots of room on the deck too. And there was a kind of little guard-house, too, to put Pee-wee in if he didn't behave. Some of the windows were broken, but I knew we could fix them easily. All we needed to do was eat some green apples and then we'd have plenty of panes. There were some lockers too, only one of them was locked and we couldn't get into it.

I guess the tramp didn't take anything, because there was nothing missing. I guess all he took was a look around. There were some cushions piled on one of the lockers and they looked as if someone had been sleeping on them.

Pee-wee said he could see the oil stove had been used by the smell—he's got such sharp eyes that be can see a smell. I told him he had a classy eye because there was a pupil in it, and you ought to have seen Mr. Donnelle laugh. I guess he thought we were crazy.

"Well we should worry about the tramp," I said, "especially now that we have a boat like this. The next thing to do is to bring the whole troop and get her fixed up."

One thing was easy anyway. Just below Bridgeboro, where we live, there is a kind of a branch flowing into the Bridgeboro River. We always called it the creek. Now we found out from Mr. Donnelle that it started along up above Little Valley. Over there they call it Dutch Creek. He said that at high tide we could float the houseboat right down into Bridgeboro River and then wait for the up tide or else tow it up to Bridgeboro. Cracky, I could see it would be a cinch ark! I was glad because we fellows didn't have money enough to have the boat carted by land. But, good night, this way was easy.

The next morning I sent a birch bark call to an the fellows in our troop. I sent them each a little piece of birch bark by courier. Connie Bennett, he's our courier. And that meant come to Special Meeting—W. S. W. S. means without scoutmaster. So pretty soon they began coming up to Camp Solitaire. That's the name I gave the tent I have on our lawn. When they were all there, I told them about Mr. Donnelle and the houseboat, and we decided that we'd hike over to Little Valley and pile right in and get it ready instead of bringing it to Bridgeboro first. We decided that if we worked on it for about three days, it would be ready.

So we all started to hike it along the road to Little Valley. We had an adventure before we got there, and I guess I'd better ten you about it. I made a map too, so you can see the way everything was. It's about five miles to Little Valley by the road.

Well, we were an hiking it along, sometimes going scout-pace and most of the time jollying Pee-wee, when all of a sudden I noticed a mark on a rock that I was sure was a scout mark. It was an arrow and it was marked with a piece of slate. Underneath the arrow was another mark like a pail, so I knew the sign meant that there was water in that direction.

I didn't know any scouts around our way that could be camping there, but whenever a scout sees a scout sign he usually likes to follow it up. So I told the fellows I was going to follow if there was any time. They said it was an old last year's mark, but go ahead if I wanted to, and I told them I'd meet them at Little Valley later. So now comes the adventure. As soon as I left the fellows, I hit the trail into the woods just like you'll see on the map I made. It wasn't much of trail and I guess a fellow couldn't follow it if he wasn't a scout. It was all thick woods like a jungle kind of, and I could see where branches had been broken by somebody that passed there. Pretty soon it began to get swampy and there wasn't any more trail at all.

As long as there's any sign of a trail you can't get me rattled, but cracky, I don't like marshes. You can get lost in a marsh easier than in any other place. Pretty soon I was plodding around deeper than my knees and it gave me a strain every time I dragged my leg out of the swamp. Maybe you'll wonder why I didn't go back, but if you do, that's because you don't know much about marshes. All of a sudden I was right in the middle of it, as you might say, and there were no landmarks at all.

Pretty soon I was in waist deep and then I was scared, you can bet. If there's one thing that gets me scared it's quicksand. As long as I could get my legs out I was all right, but when I began sinking as low as my waist and had to drag myself out by squirming and catching hold of bushes and things, then I lost my nerve — I have to admit it.

I saw I was a fool ever to go into that pesky place, but it was too late and I knew that pretty soon I'd be in too deep to get out. Oh, jiminies, I was scared. Once, after I scrambled out I tried lying flat on the marsh with the reeds laid over sideways underneath me. But they didn't hold me up and anyway I knew I couldn't lie that way forever. I wondered how a scout had ever gone through here.

Before I knew how to swim I came mighty near to getting drowned and I got lost in the woods, too, when I was a tenderfoot. But this was worse than anything I ever knew before. Once I sank down almost to my shoulders and I guess I would have been a goner, only my feet struck something hard and flat and I stood on that until I got rested a little.

All the while I looked around to see if I could decide where the land might be a little harder, but I guess I must have been in the worst part of it. I decided that the safest thing I could do was to stand just where I was. I didn't know what it was I was standing on, but anyway it didn't seem to sink any, so I was kind of safe there, as you might say. But I knew I could never raise myself out of that place and I'd have to just stand there till I got so tired and hungry, that I'd drop down and be sucked into the marsh.

So anyway, I'd have to die, I was sure of that only I didn't want to die any sooner than I had to. Two or three times I shouted as loud as I could, but I knew it wasn't any use, because I was two or three miles away from any house. Even if anybody knew, I didn't see how they could get to me and it was only by good luck that I wasn't dead already on account of the hard thing I was standing on. Every once in a while bubbles would come up and I thought it was because that thing I was standing on was sinking lower. The marsh was just about even with my shoulders and I kept looking sideways at my shoulders all the time, so as to see if I was going down any and sometimes I thought I was. But I guess I wasn't.

The weeds stood up all around me so I couldn't see, except up in the air and it was like being in a grave with just my head out. Gee, I thought about the fellows hiking it to Little Valley and beginning work on the house-boat and waiting for me to come, and I could just kind of hear them jollying Pee-wee, and oh, I wished I was there. I was wondering who the Silver Foxes would elect for their patrol leader and then I got to thinking how nobody, not even my mother and father, would ever know what became of me, because you can't drag a marsh like you can a river. And it seemed kind of funny like, to die without anybody ever knowing what became of you.

Pretty soon my legs began getting very tired like a fellow's legs always do when he keeps standing in water. Only this was worse than water. I wondered how it would feel when my knees gave out and I sank down.

Then I happened to think about having my hikebook with me. It was all wet and the pencil was wet too, but I held it up high out of the marsh and wrote this on one of the pages. After I wrote it I stuck it up high on one of the marsh weeds.

This is where Roy Blakeley, patrol leader, Silver Fox Patrol, Bridgeboro Troop, B. S. A., was sucked down into the marsh, after he couldn't stand up any more. I was standing on something that was hard and maybe you'll find my body lying on that. In my desk is something I was going to give my mother for a birthday present. I send her a lot of love too. My father too. And I hope my Patrol gets along all right and that the troop has a lot of fun this summer. I hope somebody will find this.

CHAPTER VI. THE TIGHT PLACE

After that I made up my mind I wouldn't think any more about living and then I was satisfied, kind of. 'Cause as long as you know you've got to die, what's the difference. They could get another fellow to lead the patrol, that's one sure thing. Mostly I cared about my mother on account of not being able to say good-bye to her. All of a sudden it seemed as if there was more water around me than before. Up to that time it was mushy, kind of, but not much water. But now it was more like water all around me and I noticed a little bunch of net moss near me. Maybe you don't know what net moss is. It's moss that grows in swamps. Well, what do you think I saw lying on that clump of net moss? Cracky, you'd hardly believe it, but it was a spark plug. And it looked funny to see it there.

If you're not a scout maybe you don't know anything about camping, but it's one of our rules not to defile the woods with rubbish and Mr. Ellsworth always told us a tomato can didn't look right in the woods. Well, jiminety, that spark plug sure did look funny lying on that piece of net moss. It floated right near my shoulder and I lifted it off and, oh, crinkums, but it made me 'think of Bridgeboro.

It was almost the same as if it was a fellow come to rescue me, as you might say. It was just because it didn't belong there, I guess. Of course, I knew it couldn't rescue me, but it reminded me of people and that kind of cheered me up a little. Then I began to think about it. I remembered what our scoutmaster said about a fellow that's drowning — that he can think as long as his head is out of water. And this was like drowning, only slower. I was wondering how that spark plug got there. It's funny how you'll think about little things like that even when you're dying.

One thing sure, no automobile ever went through there, and no motorcycle either. Maybe a fellow in an airplane might have dropped it, or maybe —

Then, all of a sudden I began to laugh. And while I was laughing some water flowed into my mouth. But I didn't care, I was feeling so good. I knew all about the whole thing now, and I felt like kicking myself only my feet were down in all that tangle of marsh. But what cared I, yo ho — and a couple of yee hees.

Oh, I was some wise little boy scout then, and I had a scout smile long enough to tie in a couple of bow knots. That spark plug was thrown out of a motor boat. I could see that the spark points were bad and somebody threw it away because it wouldn't work and then put in a new one. And I knew that already the tide was beginning to come up and that pretty soon there would be a creek here and that I could swim in it.

Cracky, you can't scare me when it's a question of swimming, for I wasn't brought up in a bath tub. Many's the time I swam across Black Lake. Water's all right, but swamps — good night! Maybe if you don't live near meadow lands you won't understand how it was. But when the tide rises twice every twenty — four hours (you learn that in the Fourth Grade), it makes creeks through the meadows and marshes. Some of them are deep enough for small motor boats even, only you've got to be careful not to stay up one of them too long or you'll get stuck till the next day. One time that happened to Ed Sanders that owned we Rascal and he was there all night, and he almost died from poison of the mosquitoes. Anyway I would have been dead before night when the mosquitoes come out — that's one good thing. I don't mean it's one good thing, but anyway you know what I mean.

Pretty soon I could push the swamp grass out of the way and swim a little. Oh, cracky, I was thankful for that tide I I knew it would keep on coming when it once started 'cause the tide never goes back on you. Of course it goes back, but you know what I mean. Sometimes if you're on a hike and telling time by the sun it'll go under a cloud. Or sometimes if you're lost and following the stars, it'll cloud up and you can't see them any more. And crinkums, a trail will go back on you sometimes. But the tide is sure. It's got to come up, and so I knew it was coming up to rescue me and I knew I was all right as soon as I saw that spark plug.

Pee-wee wanted to name this chapter "Saved By A Spark Plug" or "The Hero Plug," but I said it sounded silly. Any way I'll never say another word against the tide. Often when I saw motor boats stuck on the flats I could hear the men in them saying things about the tide—oh, gee, you ought to have heard some of the things they said.

But I'll never say anything, anyway. It seemed kind of, you know, like an army coming to rescue me, slow but sure, and pretty soon I was swimming around, and oh, didn't I feel good!

All of a sudden like, there was a little river there and it kept getting deeper and wider and I knew it began away out in the ocean and it seemed as if it was picking its way all the way up into these marshes, to give me a chance to do what every scout knows how to do—swim.

Of course I was saved, but I didn't know how far I'd have to swim, only I was pretty sure I wouldn't have to die now.

I guess now you'd better look at the map I made, and then you'll see how the creek came in the marshes and about where I was, when it began, to rise.

Of course I didn't know where it came from or where it went, but I decided to swim against the tide for two reasons. First I was afraid to go the other way because it might just peter out, like most of those meadow creeks do, and then I'd be in the marsh again. Oh, boy, safety first. I'd had enough of marshes. Besides if I swam the other way it would be deeper and wider and I'd be more likely to find a board or a log or something and pretty soon I might come to solid shores.

But before I started I had another adventure. I took off my shoes and stockings and everything except my underclothes. But of course, that wasn't the adventure. It was a dandy adventure, but you have to wait, and if it rains to-morrow so we can't go trailing, I'll write some more. I think it'll rain to-morrow.

CHAPTER VII. WEETONKA, THE TERRIBLE CHIEF

Of course you can tell when you look at the map where the creek came from. It came from Dutch Creek and Dutch Creek flows into the Bridgeboro River, and Bridgeboro River rises in the northern part of some place or other and takes a—some kind of a course—and flows into New York Bay. Once I got kept in, in school, for not knowing that. But how should I know where this creek went? It came-that was enough for me. I should worry where it went.

Before I started to swim I decided I'd go under and try to find out what it was that I'd been standing on. Because I had to thank it. A boy scout is supposed to be grateful. So I ducked and groped around in the marshy bottom and I felt something hard with a point to it. I had to come up for air, then I ducked again and felt around over it and under it. I joggled it with both my hands and it budged-not much but a little. Then I came up for air and went down and gave a good tug at it.

I guess it was just kind of caught in the mud and weeds for after I pulled some of these away a lot of bubbles came up, and then I got hold of one end of the thing and it stuck up slantingways out of the water like an alligator's mouth. Oh, gee, it was all slimy and had moss growing to it and it was black and hard. I was crazy to find out what it was and I swam around the end of it, bobbing it up and down. Then I sat on it and rocked it and it joggled. When I straddled it, it went down with me and when I jerked it, it seemed to get loose a little. The end that was sticking up wasn't very big around, only it was terribly slippery. Anyway, I sat on it and tightened my legs around it just like a fellow does with a balky horse, and then I began jouncing up and down like on a seesaw.

Pretty soon the other end came up and, oh, boy, didn't I get dumped off into the water. It looked like a slimy old log floating. I gave it a turn and then—g—o—o—d night—what do you think it was? It was a regular Indian dug-out.

I guess maybe it was a hundred years old and you can see it now, if you ever come to Bridgeboro, because it's in the Museum of our Public Library and you'll know it because it's got "Presented by 1st Bridgeboro Troop, B. S. A.," on it. I guess maybe it was about fifteen feet long and as soon as I cut into it with my scout knife, I saw that it was made of cedar and it wasn't rotten—not so much, anyway. Jiminies, that's one good thing about cedar; it lasts forever under water.

Oh, boy, wasn't I excited. I swam around it washing it off with my scout jacket, then I bailed the little dug out part out with my scout hat. It wasn't so black when I got it all cleaned off. It was kind of chocolate color and I knew it must be very old, because cedar turns that color after a long time. You learn that in Woodcraft. It was all made out of one piece and the place where you sit was just hollowed out—about big enough for one person.

Then I got inside and it was crankier than a racing shell. You had to sit up straight like a little tin soldier to keep it from tipping—it was one tippicanoe, you can bet. I fell out and had to roll it over and bail it out two or three times. At last I got the hang of it and I pushed it in the marshes a little way so it wouldn't drift up stream. There was a regular creek there now, good and wide and deep, and the water was coming up like a parade.

Then I pulled a lot of reeds and bound them together with swamp grass. That was a funny kind of a paddle I guess, but it was better than nothing and anyway I decided to wait till the tide was at flood and then paddle back with it. That would be a cinch.

So then I sat in the dug-out and just waited for the tide to come up. The dug-out stayed where it was on account of being pushed in among the reeds and oh, jiminety, it was nice sitting there. I thought maybe the creek would empty out again into Bridgeboro River and I could tie up there and, go home. But I had a big surprise waiting for me, you can bet.

It was about nine o'clock in the morning when I started on that crazy trail and it was about five o'clock in the afternoon when the tide began to turn and go back. All the while I was sitting there waiting I thought about the

Indian that owned that canoe. Maybe his bones were down underneath there, I thought. Ugh, I'd like to see them. No, I wouldn't. Maybe he was on his way to a pow-wow, hey?

Well, after a while when the tide turned I started paddling down. A little water came through a couple of deep cracks, but not much and I sopped it up with my hat. But oh, jingoes, I never had to sit up so straight in school (not even when the principal came through the class-room) as I did in that cranky old log with a hole in it. And oh, you would have chucked a couple of chuckles if you'd seen me guiding my Indian bark with a bunch of reeds. Honest, they looked like, a street sweeper's broom.

After a while the creek began to get wider and then I could see far ahead of me the roof of a house. Then, all of a sudden, I heard somebody shout.

"Don't bother to plug the hole up, leave it the way it is, so if the water comes in, it can get out again."

Then I heard a voice shout, "You're crazy!" and I knew it was the fellows jollying Pee-wee Harris and they were talking about a hole in the boat, because that was the roof I saw. So then I knew I was coming out into Dutch Creek right where it passes Little Valley.

Oh, boy! Wasn't I excited? Pretty soon I could see the boat and some of the fellows on it working away, sawing and hammering and jollying each other, the way the fellows in our troop are always doing. You can see by the map just how I got to where they were. I guess I must have been as near as fifty feet before Connie Bennett threw down his hammer and shouted. "Look who's here!"

Westy Martin was sitting on the edge of the deck dangling his feet and eating a sandwich. Well, you ought to have seen them all stare.

"What in the dickens do you call this?" Wig Weigand hollered.

But I didn't say a word till I got right close to them, then I gave Westy a good swat with my reed paddle.

"I am Weetonka, the famous Indian chief!", I shouted, "and I haven't had anything to eat since eight o'clock. Give me that sandwich or I'll scalp you!"

CHAPTER VIII. RESOPEKITWAFTENLY

This chapter and the next one are mostly about Wigley Weigand, but we usually call him Wig-Wag Weigand, because he's a cracker-jack on wig-wag signalling. He's good on all the different kinds of signalling. He's a Raven, but he can't help that, because there wasn't any Silver Fox Patrol when the Raving Ravens started.

The Ravens were the—what do you call it—you know what I mean—nucleus of the troop. That's how it started. There are about half a million scouts in America and all of them can't be Silver Foxes, even if they'd like to.

Wig has the crossed flags—that's the signalling badge, and the fellows say he can make the sky talk. Believe me, he can make it shout. He isn't so bad considering that he's a Raven and there's one good thing about him anyway—and that's that his mother always gives us cookies and things when we go on a hike. I got a dandy mother, too, and maybe you'll see how much I think about her, kind of, in the next chapter. Anyway I have to thank Wig Weigand, that's one sure thing.

Now maybe you think I did a good stunt in that marsh, but a scout doesn't get credit unless he uses his brains and does everything all right. And that's where I fell down, and it came near making a lot of trouble, believe me.

Many's the time Tom Slade (he's in the war now) told me never to leave a scout sign after it wasn't any more use. "Scratch 'em out," he said, "because even if it means something now, it might not mean anything six months from now." Jiminy, that fellow has some brains. He said, "Never forget to take down a sign when it's no use anymore." Well, when I found I wasn't going to die a terrible death (that's what Pee-wee called it) I didn't have sense enough to take away that note that I stuck on the reeds. When I stuck it there I reached up as high as I could, So even when the tide was high up there, I guess it didn't reach it. I was so excited to find I could get away that I never thought anything about it. And when I sailed into Little Valley in my Indian canoe, gee, I had forgotten all about it.

I found that the troop had done a good day's work caulking the hull up and slapping a couple of coats of copper paint on it, while the tide was out. So then we decided that as long as the tide was going down, we'd float her down with it to the Bridgeboro River and then wait for the up tide to float her upstream to Bridgeboro. We decided that we'd rather fix her up in Bridgeboro. So you see that this chapter is about the tide, too. Mr. Ellsworth and Mr. Donnelle both told me that I must have plenty of movement in my story, so I guess the tide's a good character for a story, because it's always moving.

Well, you ought to have seen those fellows when I sailed in shouting that I was Weetonka, the famous Indian chief. Doc Carson dropped his paint brush on Connie Bennett and he was splashed all over with copper paint— good night!

"Where did you get that thing," Pee-wee shouted, "it looks like a horse's trough."

"You have to part your hair in the middle to ride in it, I can tell you that," I told him.

"Where were you all the time?" he said.

"I was captured by a band of Apaches," I said.

"What kind of a band?" Pee-wee yelled.

"A brass band," I told him; "a brass band of Apaches."

"You make me sick!" he said, kind of disgusted.

"They took me to their village and were going to burn me at the stake, only the butcher didn't bring it, then they decided they'd chop me to pieces only the butcher didn't bring the chops—"

Oh, boy! you should have seen that kid. He fired a wet bailing sponge at me and I dodged it and it hit one of his own patrol—kerflop! I guess you'll think all us fellows are crazy, especially me. I should worry. I told them I escaped in the canoe and all that kind of stuff, but at last I told them the real story and you can bet they were glad I was saved. They all said I had a narrow escape, and I admit it was only about an inch wide.

Now, I have to tell you about how we floated the house-boat down to Bridgeboro River, and maybe you'd better look at the map, hey? Oh, but first I want to tell you about the name we gave it. Some name! We christened it with a bottle of mosquito dope. It's regular name was all rubbed off, so we decided we'd vote on a new name.

This is the way we fixed it. Each patrol thought of a name and then we mixed the three names up and made one name out of them. Then you just add a little sugar and serve.

The Ravens voted the name Sprite, the Elks voted the name Fly and the Silver Foxes voted the name Weetonka, on account of me. Then we wrote all these letters down and mixed them all up and arranged them every which way, till we got this name:

RESOPEKITWAFTENLY

Oh, boy, some laugh we had over that name. We were all sitting around in the two cabin rooms and believe me, it was some giggling match.

"It sounds like a Bolshevik name," Westy Martin said.

"You wait till the infernal revenue people get that name," I said, "it'll knock'em out." Because, of course, I knew we'd have to send the name to the infernal revenue people—I mean internal or eternal or whatever you call it—because you have to do that to get your license number.

"It's a good name," I said, "you don't see it every day."

"Thank goodness for that," Doc Carson said, It's as long as a spelling lesson or Pee-wee's tongue."

"It'll be a pretty expensive name; it'll take a lot of paint," Brick Warner said.

"We should worry," I said.

So then I made some coffee, because I'm the troop cook, and we thought it was best to eat before we started. That bunch is always hungry.

They said it was punk coffee, but that was because they didn't bring enough to go around.

"Don't laugh at the coffee," I told them, "you may be old and weak yourselves some day." I made some flapjacks, too, and then we started.

We didn't have to do much work because the ebb was running good and strong, and we just sat around the deck with our feet dangling over, and pushed her off with our scout staffs whenever she ran against the shores. She didn't keep head on, but that was no matter as long as she went, and pretty soon (I guess it must have been about seven o'clock) we went waltzing into Bridgeboro River.

And then was when we made a crazy mistake.

Just for a minute we forgot that the tide would be running down the river instead of up. If we had only remembered that, three or four of us could have gone ashore with a rope and tied her in the channel, which ran along the near shore. Then all we would have had to do would have been to sit around and wait for it to turn, so we could drift up to Bridgeboro with it.

But just when we were floating out of the creek, we forgot all about what the tide would do to us, unless we were on the job and sure enough it caught us and sent us whirling around and away over on to the flats.

"Good night!" I said when I heard her scrape.

"We should have had sense enough to know the tide is stronger here than in the creek," they all said.

"What's the difference?" Dorry Benton said,

"We're stuck on the flats, that's all. Now we don't have to bother to tie her. When the tide changes, we'll float off and go on upstream all right. We're just as well off as if we were tied up in the channel."

Well, I guess he was right except for what happened pretty soon. So we settled down to wait for the tide to go down and change. After a while we began to see the flats all around us and there wasn't any water near us at all—only the water in the channel away over near the west shore. We were high and dry and there wasn't any way for a fellow to get away from where we were, because he couldn't swim and he'd only sink in the mud, if he tried to walk it.

Well, while we were sitting around trying to figure out how long it would be before the water would go down and then come up enough to carry us off, Doc Carson said, "Listen!" and we heard the chug of a motor boat quite a long way off.

It was getting dark good and fast now, and there was a pretty wide stretch of flats between us and the channel. Pretty soon we could hear voices—all thin, sort of, as if they came from a long way off. That's the way it is on the water.

"She's coming down Dutch Creek," one of the fellows said. After a while another fellow said he thought it was Jake Holden. Then another one said it wasn't.

"Sure it is," Connie Bennett said, "listen."

Then as plain as day I could hear the words "Crab running," and then in a minute something about "bad news." Pretty soon, through the steady chugging I could hear a voice say very plain, "I'm glad it doesn't have to be me to tell her."

We couldn't make them out because it was getting too dark, but it was Jake Holden, the fisherman, all right. Pretty soon the engine began chugging double, sort of, and I knew they were going around the corner into Bridgeboro River, because there's a steep shore there, and it makes an echo.

I was a chump not to realize what they were talking about, but they had chugged around into Bridgeboro River and were heading upstream before it popped into my thick head. And even then it was on account of

35

something else they said, as the chugging grew fainter all the time. It seemed as if I heard it while I was dreaming, as you might say. I knew they were pretty far upstream by now, but the voice was awful clear, like voices always sound across the water, especially in the night.

"He was a nice little fellow," that's what I said, "but he had a right to keep out of that place."

Then, all of a sudden, I knew. They were talking about me. They must have been up that creek fishing and found that note of mine. And they were going to tell my people as soon as they got home.

"Holler to them, fellows!" I said; "quick-all together."

I guess the fellows must have thought I was crazy, but they hollered for all they were worth. But it was no use, for nobody answered. I guess the wind must have been blowing our way or something—anyway, they didn't pay any attention. Then pretty soon I couldn't hear the chugging any more at all.

Oh, jiminies, but I felt bad. Maybe you think that as long as I escaped and would get home all right I ought to be satisfied. But that's because you don't know anything about my mother. When my brother died I saw how she acted and the doctor said she had to stay in bed two or three days on account of her heart being not just right. Maybe he thought it would stop, I guess. And gee, I didn't want her to hear any bad news, even if it wasn't true. 'Cause I knew just how she'd act—I could just see her, sort of. I guess I was kind of thinking about it and how it would be when Jake Holden went to the house, and how she'd have to wait five or six hours, maybe till morning, before she saw me, when all of a sudden I heard Will Dawson of my patrol say, "What's the matter, Blakey?"—he always calls me Blakey. But I didn't pay any attention to him, because I couldn't speak—exactly. I didn't seem to see any of the troop, I only just saw my mother standing, maybe kind of unsteady like, and listening to Jake Holden.

36

Then all of a sudden I walked straight over to where the Ravens were all sitting on the cabin roof. And I spoke to Wigley Wig-wag Weigand.

I said—this is just what I said—I said, "Wig, I always claimed Ralph Warner was the best signaler in the troop and maybe you'll remember I was mad when you got the badge. But now I ain't mad, and I ain't jealous, only I don't want those men to go and tell my mother I'm dead—I—I don't. I forgot to take the note away and they're going to tell her and she—she has—her heart isn't very strong like. There's only one fellow in the troop can do it—it's you. You can do it. You can do anything, signalling. I've got to admit it now, when I need you. You're a Raven, but I want you to signal, quick. They'll see it in town. You're the only fellow can do it—you are. I got to admit it."

He didn't say much because he isn't much on talking. He's always studying the Handbook. But he jumped down and he just said, "I'll fix it." And I knew he would.

CHAPTER IX. THE LOST LETTER

Then Elmer Sawyer (he's a Raven) came up to me and said, "He'll do it, Roy; don't worry. And they'll get it too, because everybody in town is out these nights looking at the searchlights down the Hudson."

That was one lucky thing. A lot of cruisers and torpedo boats were down in the harbor and up the Hudson, and we could see their searchlights even in Bridgeboro.

Wig looked all around the cabin as if he was hunting for something and then he said, "No searchlight, I suppose." If we had only had a searchlight it would have been easy, but there wasn't any on board.

"Don't you care," Pee-wee said to me, "he'll think of a way." Oh, jiminy, but he was proud of Wig. I could see that Wig was thinking and for just a few seconds it seemed as if he couldn't make up his mind what to do.

"Can you smudge it?" Connie Bennett asked.

"Guess so," he said, "you fellows rip open the ends of these cushions, but don't tear the covering any, and somebody get the stove cleared out; see if there's a damper in the pipe, and see if there's any bilge under the flooring. It'll take those fellows about twenty minutes to chug up to Bridgeboro."

Well, in two seconds he had us all Hying every which way, Elks, Silver Foxes and all. We didn't have to open more than one of the seat cushions and, lucky thing, we found it full of excelsior. That makes a good smudge.

"Only you've got to treat it," Wig said.

"Treat it!" I said; "I'll treat it to all the ice cream it can eat, if it'll only help you to send the message." I was feeling good now.

"Take it down in the bilge and treat it," he said, very sober like, to one of his patrol.

"Don't let it spend a cent," I called after him.

But I didn't go because I could see he would rather have Ravens help him. You can't blame him for that. In about half a minute they came upstairs and they had a lot of the excelsior all damp, but not exactly wet, and I don't know how they got it that way, except I know there was bilge water down under the flooring. They're a lot of crackerjacks on signalling, I'll say that much for them. There was a stove in the main cabin with a stovepipe going straight up through the roof like a smoke stack and there was a damper in it right near the stove.

"Get a handbook or a pocket code," somebody said, "so he'll have the signs right near him."

"He doesn't need any signs," Pee-wee shouted, disgusted like.

Well, this is the way Wig did it, and after he got started, most of us went up on the roof to see if we could read it. But that's mighty hard to do when you're right underneath it.

By the time the fellows came upstairs with the damp excelsior (that's what they call the smudge) Wig had a good fire started in the stove.

"Lay that stuff down here," he said; then he said to me, "What do you want to say?"

"Just say I'm safe, Wig," I told him. "Say for them not to pay any attention to what they hear."

I only waited long enough for him to get started, just so as to see how he did it, then I went up on the roof and watched the long black smoke column. Cracky, I was glad it was moonlight, that's one sure thing.

As soon as he had a good fire started he stuffed some of the damp excelsior in and shut the door, and told Artie Van Arlen (he's their patrol leader) to hold a rag over the crack in the door, because the black smoke was pouring out that way, especially because the damper in the pipe was shut.

I didn't stay there long, because the smoke was too thick for me and when I saw Artie bind a wet rag over Wig's eyes and mouth, I knew then it was going to be mighty bad in that little cabin.

"Have another ready," I heard him say; "better have three or four of them."

Then he put his hand on the damper in the pipe and turned it and then the smoke in the cabin wasn't so bad. He just turned it around quick and kept turning it around and that let little puffs of smoke through, and I heard the fellows up on the roof shouting, "Hurrah!" so I knew it was working all right. He sent up a lot of little puffs like that, just so as to draw attention, and he; kept doing it so long I got impatient.

"No use talking till you know somebody's listening," he said, kind of pleasant like to me. I guess maybe he never liked me very much, because I didn't want that badge to get into their patrol and anyway he's kind of sober, sort of, and maybe he thought I had too much nonsense. But, oh, boy, I was strong for him now...and I could see how he began to cough and I was worried.

Then he groped around to get hold of the damper, for he was blindfolded and the smoke in there was getting thicker and thicker. Then he gave it a quick turn, then waited a few seconds, then held it lengthwise with the pipe for about twenty seconds.

"R," I said to myself.

Then he opened the damper three times, each about twenty seconds, and I could hear the fellows up on the roof shouting.

"O! It's a good O! Bully for Wig Weigand!"

"Give me another towel, quick," he said to Artie. "Is the window open? you better go up, Kid."

It was the first time he ever called me kid and he had to cough when he said it. But I just couldn't move. There was something in my throat and my eyes that wasn't smoke, and I said, "I can stand it if you can—Wig."

40

"Go on up, kid," he said, "we've—got—got—her—talking—now," and he coughed and choked.

"Go on up, Roy," Artie Van Arlen said.

Up on the roof all the fellows were sitting 'round the edge with their legs over, watching the black column in the sky, and shouting when they read the letters. But I was thinking about those fellows down in that cabin filled with smoke and how they were doing that all on account of me.

"Pretty smoky down there," one of the Elks said to me.

"You said something," I told him.

"He's marking up the sky all right, if he can only stick it out," another fellow said. "Who's down there with him ?"

"Artie," I said.

"They'll stick it out, all right," Westy Martin said; "it's easier for Artie, he can stay near the window ."

"Bully for you, Wig, old boy!" somebody shouted, just as the E in SAFE shot up. And I knew what it meant—it meant that the words Roy is safe had been printed in great big black letters across the sky.

Then it came faster and faster and it seemed as if he must be turning that damper like a telegraph operator moves his key. "Don't worry!" it said, "reports false," "Roy Blakeley safe," "Roy safe," "Blakeley alive." He said it all kinds of different ways.

Once Artie came up coughing and choking and watched a few seconds to see if the wind was blowing the smoke away as fast as the signs were made, because that was important.

"It's lucky we have that wind," he said, and then went down again in a hurry.

Pretty soon we could see some searchlights far away and I guess they were on the ships. But ours was different and nearer to Bridgeboro, and people

41

would be sure to see it, only maybe they wouldn't understand it and that's what made me worry. I'm good on reading smudge signals, even though I never sent many and I never have to have the handbook when I read the code, that's one thing. And I didn't pay much attention to all the talking and yelling, only kept my eyes up in the sky, watching that long smoky column. It beat any searchlight you ever saw. "Roy alive"—"Roy alive" it kept saying and sometimes "don't worry."

I didn't see how any fellow could manage a smudge and send it so fast and keep his spaces. The last word before it stopped was SAFE, or that's what it was meant to be, only the short flash for E didn't come. The fellows all began shouting when there wasn't any more, and I heard Pee-wee shout downstairs, "Aren't you going to put the name of the boat?"

"Do you want him to crack the sky open?" I heard a fellow say, and they all laughed.

But I remembered how that last E didn't come and I started down the ladder for all I was worth. I scrambled around the narrow part of the deck to the window and called, but nobody answered. The smoke was coming out thick.

"Wig," I said, "are you there? Are you all right? Artie, where are you?"

I had to turn away my face on account of the smoke. I pulled off my scout scarf and tied it over my mouth, so that it covered my ears too. Then I looked in and down low, because I knew that the smoke wouldn't be so thick near the floor. And I saw Wig Weigand lying there right under the stove pipe and his hand was reaching up holding the damper, and his hand was all white like and his eyes were wide open and staring. Then I shouted for all I was worth.

"Doc! Come down—hurry! Send Doc Carson down, Wig Weigand is dead—he's suffocated."

CHAPTER X. THE RAVENS

Doc Carson is a Raven and he's our First Aid Scout. He always has some things with him, because that's our rule. But you can bet I didn't wait for him. And I didn't care if I was killed or not, I didn't, if Wig Weigand was killed.

So I jumped right through the window and the smoke got into my eyes and made my ears ring, but I didn't care. I could taste it all thick, too, but I didn't care. That was the smoke that had to do what Wigley Weigand told it to, and he scribbled all over the sky with it, that's what he did, and now it had turned around and killed him.

I knew that up to six or seven inches from the floor there is never much smoke and I knew he must have lain down low when he was almost unconscious and worked that damper. And those fellows up there had been laughing and cheering all the while, when he was lying there like that.

I didn't see Artie anywhere and there wasn't any sound. I lay down flat and crawled over to Wig and you bet I worked quick. I tied his hands together with my scout scarf—it was the Silver Fox scarf—and I tied the scarf around my neck.

"Wig," I said, but he didn't speak and his legs and his neck hung loose, sort of, and it kind of scared me. Then I crawled to the window, because I couldn't see the door, dragging him after me. Then I did something I never thought I could do, but maybe you've noticed you can do most anything when you have to. I just stood up, then fell down again, coughing and choking, and my ears were buzzing all the time. But I didn't care, I just stood up again with him hanging to me, and I grabbed the window sill and dragged him half way across it and with his head outside, and then I staggered and tried to grab something and my eyes were stinging and, oh, I don't know, all of a sudden my head knocked and I didn't know any more.

Mr. Ellsworth says that Doc ought to write the rest of this chapter, but he wouldn't, and it's just like him. The next thing I knew I was sitting on the lowest step and Connie Bennet was holding my head. "You're all right," he said, "but you got a good bump. You were only there a few seconds."

"Did you pull me out?" I said. "Where's, Wig?"

"Doc brought him around," he said, "he got him breathing, then it was easy. We couldn't find Artie."

Maybe it was funny, but just then I didn't seem to be thinking about Artie. I felt my head and found I had a big bump on it.

"I should worry about that," I said. "Where's Wig?"

Then I got up and went around the cabin to the forward deck and there were all the fellows and Wig sitting up and Doc Carson holding him and moving: him, so as to keep him breathing — scout fashion.

"All righto, kid," Doc said, kind of pleasant, "you're a brick."

I always thought; that I was as big as he was, but he called me kid, and I didn't care. Anyways I couldn't see him very good, I admit that. Because — oh, well, maybe you can understand.

"Artie's missing," he said. "You didn't see anything of him in there?"

"I couldn't see at all, hardly," I told him.

Then Wig turned his head and looked at me and he was all white and weak looking, especially when he smiled. And he had the remains of my Silver Fox scarf, all torn, around his neck.

"All right?" he said very low.

But I just couldn't speak to him. I don't know what made me do it, but I went up to him and he looked at the bump on my forehead and said, "Hurt?"

"You should worry about that," I told him.

44

Then I kind of fixed the Silver Fox scarf better, so that it was around his neck and I tied it in the Silver Fox knot. "Your fellows won't mind if you wear it a little while," I said, and then I unfastened his own scarf, yellow and brown, and tied it around my neck. "There's no fellow can get this away from me to-night," I said, "I'm going to wear the Raven scarf—I am."

Then, all of a sudden, I noticed that Doc had gone away and I was holding his head up alone. So I let it down on the cushion very easy and I saw we were all alone. Maybe you won't understand and it's hard to tell you. But I didn't say anything; I just stayed there and rubbed his forehead.

"We told her," he said, kind of as if he was weak and tired.

"Yup," I said, "you told her"

"Somebody'll get it—maybe," he said.

"I ain't thinking about that," I said, "I'm only thinking about how you did it, I—I don't want the signalling badge in my patrol now, honest I don't, Wig. I want it to stay where it belongs. And I want there to be only just the one in the troop. I got mad first. That's because I'm always getting mad, I guess. But there will never be any signalling badge in my patrol, Wig. That's going to be the rule."

"There'll be a Gold Cross though," he said. And then he shut his eyes.

But I stayed right there—just because—oh, I don't know, just because I wanted to stay right there. You can't always tell why you want to do a thing.

CHAPTER XI. LOST

Now when Wig said that about the Gold Cross I thought it was just because he was weak and didn't know what he was saying. Because, maybe you know as well as I do, that the Gold Cross isn't so easy to get. Only one fellow in our troop ever got it, and that was Tom Slade. Maybe I took a chance when I went into all that smoke, I'm not saying I didn't, but if I got anything at all, it would be the Bronze Medal, I guess, but nix on the Gold Cross. You don't find gold crosses growing around on every bush, you can bet. Anyway, I didn't want any honor medal because I knew Wig wouldn't get one (because they're only for lifesaving) and gee, if he didn't deserve one, I'm sure I didn't.

Anyway this wasn't any time to be thinking about medals, because Artie Van Arlan was missing and that was the principal thing we had to think about. He wasn't on the house — boat, that was one sure thing, because we looked everywhere and couldn't find him. Wig said he remembered somebody speaking to him when he was lying there, and he guessed it must have been Artie. He didn't know what he said though.

The fellows were all excited about it, especially because the boat was just beginning to float, and we didn't know whether we'd better anchor there and wait to see if he turned up. Two of the fellows climbed down and swam around and the rest kept caning. It wasn't very deep yet and they could even feel around the flats, but they couldn't find him anywhere.

I went around and looked at the window and even then the cabin was filled with smoke, but not so thick. Believe me, I wished that Tom Slade was there then, because he's great on deducing and finding clues and all like that. That's why we always called him Sherlock Nobody Holmes. Anyway, I couldn't make out what happened. Artie might have staggered up against the window to get air, but I didn't see how he could fall out, and if he was able to climb out then why didn't he come up where the rest of us were?

I couldn't make anything out of it; all I knew was he was gone. I knew he must have been drowned and his body been carried up by the tide, which was running up strong now.

Well, you can bet we didn't have any fun drifting up. Nobody said anything much; we just sat around the edge of the deck with our staffs and pushed her off, whenever she ran against the shore.

Charlie Seabury sat next to me and after a while he said, "Who's going to tell his people?"

"I am," I told him, "because I'm to blame for the whole business."

"Nobody's to blame," he said.

"Yes, I am," I said, "they just did it on account of me."

"That's because all the fellows like you," he said, "and they like to do anything for you."

Anyway, it wasn't so necessary, I see that now, and it's just the same as if I killed him. Gee, I wish it was I that got killed, I know that. Cracky, I deserved to after being such a fool.

After that, nobody spoke for a long time, then Hunt Ward, who's in the Elk Patrol, said, "It's the first fellow in our troop that died. I guess we won't go up to camp now."

"Not in this boat, anyway," I said.

Then after a while I said, "We'll send his name in and they'll print it in Boys' Life."

"I know," Hunt said, "with a black line around it."

Yet we kind of kept hoping all the time, even though we knew there wasn't any sense in it. "You thought you were a goner," Hunt said, "and you came back all right."

Now I was a big fool that it didn't put a certain idea in my head when he said that, but I only said, "Yes, but that was different."

Then Dorry Benton, who was two or three fellows away from me, said, "One thing is sure, he went through the window and into the water. Maybe he was half conscious and didn't remember there was only a narrow strip of deck there. And he must have tumbled right off it."

"I don't know," I said, "only if he isn't in the boat then he must be in the water and if he fell in the water and couldn't swim or shout either, then he must be drowned."

Then nobody said anything and we just sat there keeping her off shore and watching her drift up. When we got around Bentley's turn we could see the lights in Bridgeboro and then was when I began to realize and I hated to get home. I wished the tide wouldn't take us so fast. Some of the fellows walked around on the roof, but none of them said anything. I wished it was me instead of Artie, I know that. I ought to have been satisfied to escape without getting the Ravens to do that—I mean send that message for me. Anyway, I made up my mind I'd be the one to tell Mr. Ellsworth about it, and Artie's people too, and I'd take all the blame.

I guess nobody said anything more all the way up, until we came near the Field Club landing. The shore is like low cliffs here and after we got her over against it, a couple of the fellows got out and towed her along with ropes, till we came to the long float.

"Are we going to tie her at the float?" Connie Bennett asked, very sober like. Gee, it sounded funny to hear someone speak. Doc Carson said, "Yes." He was kind of like head of the three patrols now, because he has the most sense of all of us, I guess, and Tom Slade, who is head of the Elks, is away and I decided, all of a sudden, that I wasn't much of a patrol leader, and Artie—he was—he wasn't there.

"Look out for that canoe," somebody said, just as we were coming alongside the float. "They shouldn't have left it there," Connie said; "that's no place for a canoe." I guess we were all kind of nervous and cranky like. Then I saw that there was a black figure sitting on the lowest step of the boathouse. I was just going to call "Who's there?" when Doc said, "Pull that canoe out of the way before we smash it in."

So I jumped off onto the float and grabbed the canoe, and g-o-o-d night! it was my Indian dugout.

CHAPTER XII. ARTIE'S ADVENTURE

Then I heard one of the fellows shouting "Look who's here!" and I saw the fellow who had been sitting on the steps coming toward the float and I could tell it was Artie Van Arlen. Then I could hear Pee-wee dancing on the cabin roof and screaming, "The plot grows thicker! The plot grows thicker!"—good night, the kid was almost having a fit.

"If it wouldn't be too much trouble," I said to Artie, "would you please relate your adventures, I see that you're not dead."

"Well, not so you'd notice it," he said, "but I guess I came pretty near it."

Then I could see he was all in and must have had a pretty hard time of it, but I couldn't help kidding him, because I was feeling so good to know he was safe. Believe me, that fellow had some adventure.

"It was lucky for me," he said, "that you tied this crazy canoe or whatever you call it-"

"That is an Indian dugout, if anyone should ask you," I said, "and if I wanted to sell it to an antiquary—"

"A what?" Pee-wee shouted down from the cabin roof.

"An antiquary," I said; "comes from the Latin word aunt and the Chinese word query, meaning to ask questions—otherwise the same as Pee-wee. As I was saying, if I wanted to sell it to an antiquary I could get a large check for it."

"How large?" Pee-wee shouted.

"About eight inches by two and a half inches; now, shut up!" I said.

Cracky, you should have heard those fellows laugh.

"Well, whatever it is," said Artie, "it's lucky for me that you tied it just under the cabin window, because I fell into it—I fell in good and hard."

"I think you fell in soft," I said; "it shows how thoughtful I am. A scout is foresighted—"

"You make me sick!" Pee-wee shouted.

"Tell Doc Carson to give you some medicine," I answered.

Laugh! Because, you see, we were all feeling so good about Artie being saved that we'd laugh at nothing, like a lot of girls. But girls are all right, I have to admit that.

Let's see, where was I? Oh, yes, I was telling you about Artie. You see when I first arrived with that canoe I tied it just under the cabin window and then scrambled up through the window. So there it was all the time. Lucky thing, too. Only the funny thing was we never missed it—we were punk scouts, that's sure.

Then Artie told us how it was. "After the smoke got so thick that I was dizzy and couldn't see, I got scared and groped around for Wig. I couldn't find him anywhere and he didn't answer. I didn't know whether all of the signal had been sent or not, but anyway I knew I couldn't stand it in there any longer. I thought Wig must have climbed out of the window. So I decided I would do the same thing. Oh, but didn't I have some job finding it! I lay down flat, I knew enough to do that anyway, and then I crawled around with one hand up feeling for the window sill. When I found it I was so dizzy I just hung to it and I thought I was a goner sure."

"I know how you felt," I said, "because I was in the same trouble myself."

Then he said how he dragged himself up to the window sill and tried to shout, but couldn't. Then he fell across it and kind of wriggled out. He didn't have his senses, but he knew enough to know that there was a narrow part of the deck, just a passageway sort of, outside, and he thought he'd fall on that. But it was lucky he didn't. He fell past it right into the water and that brought him to his senses, kind of. So he sputtered and groped around till he happened to clutch the Indian dugout and it rolled over with him and the anchor that we had laid in it with a rope to hold it fast to the houseboat, the anchor rolled out, and the first thing he knew he was drifting up the river, hanging onto the dugout for dear life.

He was feeling so weak and sputtering so on account of his lungs being all filled with smoke, that he couldn't shout and after a while he drifted up on the bar near Second Bend. Then he got the dugout set right side up on the mud while he bailed it out by splashing in it with his hands and afterwards making them into a cup.

After that it was easy drifting up stream and when he got to about a quarter of a mile below the boathouse, he managed to paddle over to the shore and then he pulled himself along by holding on to the weeds and things.

"You had a pretty narrow escape," Pee-wee said.

"It was a narrow boat, why shouldn't he have a narrow escape," I said; "I had a good wide escape, anyway."

"Didn't you have your hat with you to bail with?" somebody asked Artie.

"All I had was my copy of Initiation Drill," he said.

"Why didn't you drill a hole in the boat then," I said.

"What for?", Pee-wee shouted.

"So the water could get out as fast as it came in".

"What are you talking about? You're crazy!" he yelled.

"There should be two holes in every boat," Connie Bennet said, in that slow way he has; "one for the water to come in and the other so it can get out."

Gee-williger! You should have seen Pee-wee.

Anyway, I suppose you think by this time that we're all crazy. I should worry.

CHAPTER XIII. TRACKING

Anyway, you can bet I didn't stay there long, because I wanted to find out if Wig's signal had been received. Maybe you won't understand, but down the river it seemed all right and I was sure somebody must have caught it. But after we landed and I started up home, it seemed as if it was just kind of playing, after all, because that's the way some people think about the scouts, so I hurried as fast as I could so that my mother and father wouldn't be worrying. I felt awfully funny, kind of, as I went up the lawn because I knew that if no one had come and told them about the signal, they'd think I was dead.

They were sitting on the porch waiting for me and I knew from the way my mother put her arms around me that they had been worrying. She asked we what had kept me so late and my father said that I ought to send them some word when I was going to stay out as late as midnight. I have to admit he was right, too.

But anyway, I knew that they hadn't received any word about me from anybody, and I was all up in the air about that. I could see that Jake Holden hadn't been there at all and that nobody had come and told them about the signal, either. I didn't exactly ask them, but I could tell it all the same. So I told them all about everything that happened, about how I got caught in the marsh and all that, and especially about Wig being such a hero. Then she cried a little, kind of, and I said there was no use crying because I was home all right. But anyway, she cried just the same, and hugged me awful tight just as if everything hadn't ended all right. That's a funny thing about mothers.

So then I went to bed and I lay awake thinking about everything that happened. What I thought about most was why Jake Holden hadn't come and told my mother and father like I heard him say he was going to do. You remember how I heard him say that. So that was a mystery—that's what Pee-wee would call it. And I was wondering why he hadn't come to the house to give them that note he had found. Because I knew Jake

Holden (he always called me "Scouty") and he liked me, too, and I knew he would sure have come to the house if something hadn't happened.

Now that I was all calmed down, as you might say, I wasn't surprised any more about no one reading the signal, because maybe it didn't show very plain in Bridgeboro and anyway, most grown people seem to think that signalling and all that kind of thing are lots of fun for scouts, but not much use except when grown people, and especially the navy, do it.

Anyway, I should worry about grown people, because we have plenty of fun.

Oh, boy, didn't I sleep that night! When I got up I made up my mind that I'd go to Jake Holden's shanty, just for the fun of it, and find out why he didn't come and tell my family that I was dead. Because, if I was dead, he sure ought to have come and told them. Of course, I knew I wasn't dead, but anyway, how did he know that? After breakfast I did my good turn—I turned my sister Ruth's bed around for her so as it faced the bay window. I was going to turn it twice and tall it two good turns, but she said that wouldn't be fair—that that wouldn't be two good turns. I said it would be just as fair as Pee-wee turning the ice-cream freezer till the cream was all frozen and then saying he did a hundred good turns. Then she threw a tennis ball at me, but it missed me. That's one thing about girls, they can't throw a ball. They can't whistle, either.

Now comes another adventure. After breakfast I went to Marshtown (that's a few houses down near the river) to Jake Holden's shanty.

It's a funny kind of a place made out of barrel staves and part of a boat all jumbled up together, and it looks kind of like a chicken coop. He lives all alone and kind of camps out. He's a nice man, you can bet, only you have to get on the right side of him. If you can't get on the right side of him the safest place is behind him. He catches fish and crabs and goes around town selling them.

He taught me how to cook.

When I got to his shanty I saw it was locked up and he wasn't anywhere around. I guess he event down the bay crabbing. Anyway, I ran as fast as I could to Marshtown landing to see if he had gone yet, but there wasn't any sign of his boat there. Maybe you think I wasn't disappointed. Anyway, I began looking around like a scout is supposed to do, to see if there were any signs to show me whether he'd be back soon, because maybe he only went up to the club landing for gasoline. But there weren't any signs and he didn't show up.

Now, if I hadn't been a scout I would have gone home and played tennis or followed the shore up to the club landing and waited for the troop to come and go to work on the houseboat. But instead of that, I kept looking around and pretty soon what do you think I saw? I saw a footprint. Some Robinson Crusoe, hey?

It was a funny kind of a footprint. It wasn't Jake's, I knew that, because he always wore fisherman's boots. It was in the soft earth near the landing and I could see it plain. I guess maybe it was made by a good shoe, because it was pointed, but it was all worn out, that was one sure thing, because there was a place that was made by a stocking or a bare foot, where there wasn't any sole at all.

Maybe you don't know much about deduction, but that's one thing scouts learn about, and I tried to make out what it meant, but it had me guessing. Because the shoe was pointed and had the remains of a rubber heel — I could tell that by the big screw holes. And that meant good shoes. And I thought it was funny anybody who could wear good shoes would let them wear out like that.

Anyway, it was none of my business, only there was one mighty funny thing about that footprint. There was an Indian's head stamped right in the mud. It wasn't very plain, but I could see it was an Indian's head all right. It was something like the Indian's head on a cent.

Oh, boy, I was all up in the air then, because I didn't understand how that could be there, Maybe you'll say that it was stamped there to show what make of shoes they were, but that's where you're wrong, because most of the sole was all worn away and the mark would be worn away, so somebody must have cut it there lately, that was one sure thing, and I couldn't understand why any body would want to cut that on an old worn-out shoe.

So I sat down on the edge of the float to think about it and then I saw two or three more just like it, and even more, too, only not all of them were so plain. Believe me, I didn't know what to think. Then all of a sudden I happened to remember that the Indian's head is the design of the scout pathfinder badge.

Jiminetty, but didn't I get down on my knees and study those some more. Maybe it didn't have anything to do with the scouts, but maybe it did.

And even if it did I couldn't make out what it meant, because that shoe was no scout shoe. I know a scout shoe when I see one, you can bet.

Anyway, I made up my mind I was going to follow that track as far as I could. Maybe it would peter out on a street or something and then — good night!

You'll see what happened in the next chapter. Oh boy, it's going to be a peacherino!

CHAPTER XIV. THE SLACKER

One thing, I wished Tom Slade was there, because he was the best tracker we ever had. He could track an airplane — that's what the fellows used to say. But he was over in France and the only other fellow in our troop who is a crackerjack at tracking, is Westy Martin. I don't say that just because he's a Silver Fox, because I have to admit that Artie Van Arlen and Wig Weigand are heroes, and they're not Silver Foxes. But, honest, Westy is a winner when it comes to tracking, and you've got to remember that, because now I'm going to tell you some other things about him and maybe you won't know just what to think. But I'm going to tell you straight just what happened.

Well, I decided that I'd rather have another fellow with me, because that's a good rule in tracking and anyway two fellows are better than one. And anyway, I knew he could hold a track longer than I could. He got the pathfinder's badge for one of the best tracking stunts that was ever done up at Temple Camp and he's done enough tracking stunts to win it two or three times over. He's a fiend on tracking.

By now I knew that the fellows would all be coming down to the boat club landing to work on the houseboat, because we had it fixed that they would all be there by nine o'clock. I wasn't going to flunk on that, you can bet, but I thought if I told them about the footprint they'd let Westy and me off for a little while, because if a scout is after a merit badge he can usually get leave all right. Anyway, that's the way it is in our troop. And all the fellows knew I had the tracking bee, all right. Gee, I hate to tell you about this, but I have to. Now, the way you get from Marshtown landing up to the boat club landing is to follow the shore and its only about a quarter of a mile. After I'd hiked it a little way, I could hear the fellows talking and sawing and hammering, and I knew they were all busy working.

When I got there they were all over the houseboat like flies, painting and varnishing and fixing up the flagpole, and I could hear Pee-wee as usual, shouting away. Jiminy, but it sounded good.

Then I could hear somebody say, "Well, well better late than never," and I saw it was our scoutmaster, Mr. Ellsworth. He took a day off to help the fellows.

"I'm only six minutes late," I said; "Silver Foxes always show up."

"Well, let us hope so," Mr. Ellsworth said

And I kind of saw that something was wrong. "Westy isn't here," somebody shouted.

"He'll be here in a minute," I said; "get to work; you should worry about Westy."

But just the same I felt sort of uncomfortable because one thing Mr. Ellsworth is a stickler about is us being on time. Whenever a scout comes late for campfire up at Temple Camp or at a troop meeting either, he always gets a look from T. E. At camp we have breakfast at 7:42 and lunch at 1:23 and supper at 7:13, just to teach the fellows to go by minutes.

Anyway, I started working with my patrol, who were painting the deck. I stuck right to it, but all the time I was wishing that Westy would show up. Every time I heard a sound I looked up. Because maybe you don't know that a patrol leader is responsible for his patrol and if one of them falls down, it's just the same as if he fell down. First the fellows kidded us about it, especially me, and spoke about the Tardy Foxes, and the Sleepy Foxes, but pretty soon Mr. Ellsworth came to me and said he guessed I'd better go into the club house and telephone to Westy and find out what was the matter.

"Find out if he's awake yet," somebody said.

"Maybe we'd better send a taxi for him," another fellow shouted.

"You think you're very funny, don't you?" I said, "Maybe you raving Ravens won't rave so much when you find out he's sick in bed." So I went in and telephoned, and oh, jiminy, that was the first time in my life that I ever really wished a fellow was sick. But his mother told me he hadn't been home since about half-past seven and that when he went out he had a catching-mitt and a baseball with him.

Jiminies, I don't often get scared, but I could feel my heart up in my mouth, kind of, and I didn't know what to tell the fellows and Mr. Ellsworth. It was like a disgrace to my patrol and it disgraced me, too, you can bet. He would go off and play ball and let us fellows do all the work on the boat and then he'd go in it up to Temple Camp. Gee, that's one thing a scout never is-mean. We had it all fixed up to work and then he flunked and let us do it all.

First I thought maybe I'd kind of not tell Mr. Ellsworth all about that phone call and say I couldn't hear very plain, and all like that. But I saw if I did that, I'd be worse than Westy. It was bad enough having a slacker in my patrol without having a liar.

No, siree!

So I just went up to him and I said, "Mr. Ellsworth, he's out playing ball somewheres and I guess he didn't intend to come. I admit it disgraces my patrol and it disgraces the whole troop. I was going to ask you if you thought maybe I could go away for an hour or so to follow a track I found, but I won't now; I'll just stay here and work twice as hard so as to make up for him. And the other fellows in my patrol will too. Maybe that will make it seem not quite so bad."

CHAPTER XV. DURING NOON HOUR

One of the things that made me feel especially bad was that Wig Weigand and Artie Van Arlen were there working, even after being nearly killed the night before, and Artie was kind of lame, too, from straining his ankle when he fell. Gee, I had to hand it to those fellows. And even Pee-wee was working away with the rest of the Ravens and running to buy nails and everything.

Both of the other patrols were all there except Tom Slade in the Elks, but they kept his place open for memory, sort of.

After a little while Mr. Ellsworth strolled over to where I was working and said to me—gee, he was awful nice the way he said it—he said, "Roy, if you want to follow up that trail you may as well go ahead and come back after lunch. We're going to hit the eats pretty soon now." That's the way he always says it, "hit the eats."

"I was expecting Westy to go with me," I told him.

"Well, no matter," he said; "Go alone and don't worry any more about Westy. It wasn't because Westy or any other single scout was needed here for we have plenty of scouts on the job, but it was just that he didn't show up when we all planned to be here, that's all. I don't like to think of any; of my scouts falling down."

"It's the same about my patrol," I said, "and I'm ashamed, that's one sure thing."

He said I shouldn't feel that way and that he guessed playing baseball was good exercise anyway. But he only said that so I wouldn't feel bad. Anyway as long as they were going to eat I thought I might as well go ahead and see if I could do that tracking if it didn't take me too far. On the way down to the other landing I thought what I'd say to Westy. I knew he'd get a troop reprimand, but I decided he'd get a patrol reprimand too, you bet. And I was feeling pretty bad about it too, because none of the Silver Foxes ever got a troop reprimand. They got patrol reprimands but not troop reprimands. And Westy had gone and spoiled it all and, gee, that's one word I don't like—slacker.

When I got to the other landing I started following that trail. If you think Westy had anything to do with it, you're mighty mistaken, because he didn't. He always wore scout shoes, I knew that.

Well, believe me, that trail was a cinch and I could follow it as easy as a clothes line. It went right up through River Lane where there isn't any pavement and every footprint was plain. I was afraid it would go through Daws Place, because that's the easiest way to get to Main Street, and I'd lose it there on account of the pavement. But it didn't, and, oh, boy, wasn't I glad! Instead of going that way the tracks went right up across the ball field, just as plain as print. That's another way to get to Main Street, and it brings you out at Harvey's candy store, but don't ever go there for ice cream cones, because you get bigger ones down at Jack's.

Then I lost the trail on account of the pavements. Gee, that's one thing I don't like about pavements. So there's where I did some deducing. Maybe you don't know what bridging a trail-gap means. You have only yourselves to blame for not being scouts. Bridging a trail-gap means stopping to think when you lose a trail. You have to decide where it most likely starts again. That's what grown-up scouts call mental tracking. So I sat down on Ridgeway's carriage step and thinked a couple of thinks. That's right on Main Street, you know, and I had to decide if that person went up or down Main Street or across the street. Right across the street is the big bank building. I've got forty-two dollars and eighteen cents interest in that bank. Mr. Temple is the head of it, and he's awful rich—he owns railroads and things. He started Temple Camp. He calls me "Curly" because my hair curls. I should worry.

Right down alongside of the bank runs Barrel Alley. It reminds you of Fifth Avenue, it's so different. That's where Tom Slade was born, down there. Most every day somebody dies down there, but anyway there are paving— stones there now, that's one good thing. Except for tracking. So you see

61

how it was that person, who ever he was, could have gone up Main Street or down Main Street, or over the stone crossing into Barrel Alley.

I decided that he went across into Barrel Alley for several reasons. One was that he went across the ball field, and that meant that he'd have to get down and crawl under the fence, so I decided it was not a grown-up person, because most of them have stiff backs and they'd rather walk a mile than crawl under a fence. They're all the time saying they're not as young as they used to be. And if it was a boy he'd be most likely to go into Barrel Alley because, believe me, they have boys down there by the dozens, especially the kind that wear worn-out shoes that rich people give them. So that accounts for the good shoes all worn out. Smart boy, hey?

So you see that's the way I bridged that trail, though I couldn't be sure I was right, I have to admit that. Anyway I went across the street and I saw by the clock in the bank that it was half past twelve. I knew I couldn't go much farther because I wanted to get back to the house-boat by one.

I started down Barrel Alley, watching the mud along the edge of the sidewalk, so I could tell if the fellow left the sidewalk to go into one of the houses. Barrel Alley is a blind alley-that means it has an end to it and you can't go any further. It runs plunk into the end of Shad Row. Norris Row is the right name, but old man Norris is named Shadley Norris, so us fellows call it Shad Row. You can get through the end of Barrel Alley if you climb over old man Norris back fence, so it isn't exactly a blind alley. It's just a little near-sighted, kind of.

Anyway I started through it and I knew if my quarry (that means the fellow you're tracking) went down there, he most likely went into one of the tenement houses and I'd see that footprint as soon as he turned off from the sidewalk.

Well, pretty soon I did see it right alongside the sidewalk just where he started to go into one of the houses. And oh, wasn't I tickled! If it hadn't been for Westy Martin and the way he'd acted I would have felt as grand as the Grand Central Station. But that was the thing I was thinking most about and when you're thinking about something like that, you don't have as much fun—I know I don't anyway.

But as long as I was there, I might as well find out who it was I had tracked and solve the mystery about the Indian head. That's the way Pee-wee would have said it, "Solve the mystery!" He gets that kind of talk out of books. The next-chapter is going to be a dandy and I promised to let him give it a name, so don't blame me whatever it is.

So long.

CHAPTER XVI. NOBLE RAGS

"Good night!" I said to Pee-wee, "what kind of rags do you call those?"

"Didn't you ever hear of noble rags?" he yelled; "that shows how much you know about story writing."

"Are they any relation to a dish rag?", I asked him.

"You think you're smart, don't you," he said; "do you know what a hero is — a ragged hero?"

"Sure, a hero is a male shero," I told him; "you learn that in the third grade. Just the same as a cowardice is a female coward."

"You make me sick!" he yelled.

"I've heard of gasoline rags and dish rags and wash rags," I kept up, "but I never saw any noble ones. Have your own way. I should worry."

"It's a good name for a chapter," he said.

"I wouldn't know a noble rag if I met one in the street," I told him. So that's how this chapter got it's name, and I don't know what it means any more than you do. I suppose the next one will be called "Trash Paper," or something like that.

Well, anyway, I stood on that doorstep for a few minutes, because I didn't know what to do next. I was sure the fellow went in there, but I didn't know where he went and anyway, I didn't, have any excuse to hunt him out because I was only tracking him for a stunt. Anyway I went in and when I got upstairs one flight I saw just a sign of that print in the ball just in front of a door. The hall was all dirty and greasy like. So by that I was pretty sure he had gone in there and you see how I tracked him all the way from Marshtown landing. Then I made up my mind that he sure wouldn't be mad if he knew I did it just for a stunt and I'd tell him I was scouting. For just a minute I was scared, then I gave a rap on the door.

Oh, but it was dark and it smelled bad in that hall. I guess they ought to tear down that row of tenements. Pretty soon I rapped again, and I felt kind of funny, because I didn't know what I ought to say—especially if a woman opened it. All of a sudden it opened very soft, and, good night I who should be standing there but—who do you think?

Westy Martin.

Jiminetty, but wasn't I flabbergasted! Even as surprised as I was, I looked down at his feet and sure enough he had on scout shoes, almost new. Talk about plots growing thicker! This one was getting so thick you couldn't drive a nail into it.

"Well—what—are—you—doing—here?" I gasped out just like that.

"Shh," he said, "keep quiet; come in, but keep quiet."

So I went in, all flabbergasted and there was a room with the paper all falling off the walls and no carpet On the floor, but anyway the windows were wide open, that was one good thing. And over in the corner was an old cot without any sheets or anything and, oh, gee, it looked bad because I've got a dandy bed up in my den—all brass and filigree work—you know.

But, crinkums, I didn't notice the cot much because there was a fellow on it and as soon as I looked at him I knew who it was, even though he looked worse than he most always did. It was Skinny McCord.

"You waked him up by knocking," Westy said

"It isn't the first knocking I did to—day," I said "but I guess I can see how it is now—I guess I can."

"It's only a good turn," he said; "he did you a good turn, and so I had to do one for him, that's all. It's for the scouts too, and I don't care what they say."

Then I happened to notice a catching mitt and a baseball over on a table near Skinny, where there was some medicine too. And then, all of a sudden, everything seemed to glisten like, especially when I blinked my eyes. Gee, I know how easy it is for girls to cry, but a fellow—anyway—when I saw Westy sit down on the edge of that cot and not pay any attention to me, only to Skinny, I couldn't speak at all. I only just happened to think to do something and I'm glad I thought about it. I just raised my hand and made Westy Martin the full scout salute. Patrol leaders don't do that mostly to the fellows in their patrols, but I should worry about rules and things like that.

"You're taking care of him?", I said as soon as I could, and I felt all foolish sort of. "I tracked him, but I never thought" — and I just couldn't say any more.

But even still Westy didn't speak to me, only he said to Skinny, "Here's a real patrol leader come to see you — that's a big honor, that is, and he just made you the full salute. You remember it in the Scout Handbook?"

"I made that salute to you," I said to Westy, all choking, I have to admit it, "and I meant it too."

"You're a great tracker," he said; "wouldn't you like to be as good a tracker as he is, Skinny?" And I could see that all he cared about was amusing Skinny.

"Don't talk about me," I said; "I'm a big fool, that's what I am, but tell me all about it."

"There isn't anything to tell," said Westy, "except that Skinny always wanted to be a scout, but he didn't have any money and all like that. But anyway, he got the Handbook and studied it all up and it got him."

"Same as it gets any fellow that looks inside of it," I said.

"And the part that interested him most of all was tracking and signalling. You see how he carved the tracking emblem on one of his shoes — "

"You needn't show it to me," I said, "I saw it."

"Last night," Westy said, "he read that smudge signal, because he learned the Morse Code out of the Handbook, and he knew that somebody might be coming up the river with the false report. He didn't know just what he ought to do and I guess he was scared to go up to your house because he didn't have any good clothes. So he ran down through the marshes and waited at the landing, because he knew Jake Holden would be coming up stream. Jake's one good friend to him, and he often took him out and he wasn't afraid of Jake.

"Pretty soon he heard Jake's boat coming up the river and saw the light and he just waited there and when Jake come up alongside the float, the first thing Skinny heard him say was, Roy Blakeley is dead—didn't you, Skinny?"

But I could see that Skinny's eyes were shut now and he didn't hear.

"Go on," I said. "So Skinny told him it wasn't true, and told him about the signal. Jake didn't pay much attention because he thought Skinny was just a little crazy on account of being so poor and hungry and all that and not having a good home. So he was going up to your house anyway and Skinny cried and hung onto him, and begged him not to. I guess he went on kind of crazy, but he said he was sure because he knew the Morse Code. Anyway, just to humor him, I guess, Jake promised him he'd wait till early in the morning, and meanwhile you came home. Do you see?"

Honest, I couldn't answer him.

"Skinny was the one who did it," he said. "That accounts for his tracks, don't you see?"

I shook my head to show him I understood. But I couldn't say it.

"And that's how tracking and signalling have brought the three of us together—see?" Westy said. "It's funny, isn't it, how it brings the three of us together here in this tenement house."

"How did you come here?" I said.

"I was just starting for the house-boat this morning early, when I met Skinny's mother. She was going to do her day's washing. And she told me how she had to leave him sick in bed, and she asked me if I'd go and stay with him till she got back. I went back and got the ball and mitt because I thought maybe he'd like them. She said he got a bad cold in the marshes and he was all excited and kind of crazy from the way he'd hung onto Jake and begged him not to go up to your house—what did the fellows think when I didn't show up?"

"You—you should worry," I just blurted out.

"Anyway I don't care so much about the troop or Mr. Ellsworth either," he said, "and even if I cared about Skinny it wouldn't do much good, because he's going to die—the doctor says so. But I care a lot about you and he did you a good turn. I was afraid he might die before you had a chance to pay him back. So I just sort of tried to pay him back for you—"

All the while he was talking I could hardly hear what he was saying and there was one word ringing through my head.

It was the word slacker.

CHAPTER XVII. THE TWO CROSSES

I guess maybe I'd better tell you about Skinny now, so you'll know all about who he is. Before I was a scout I used to call him Wash-board, because he was so skinny you could have used his ribs for a wash-board. I guess I used to think that was funny, but, gee, when you get to be a scout you find out what real fun is and you don't call names like that.

He always lived down in Barrel Alley and his mother goes out washing. Once Skinny's father hit him on the head and it made him queer like. But he got better mostly. Only he was always afraid of people after that. His father went away and got killed. Sometimes Skinny sold papers at the station, but he was always scared of people, especially rich fellows. How should I know he was interested in Scouts? He didn't have much to eat, I guess. Anyway Jake Holden was a good friend to him and he wasn't scared of Jake. I guess maybe he had consumption.

He didn't wake up again then, anyway he didn't open his eyes, and as soon as his mother came home from her work Westy and I went home. I wasn't thinking anything about the house-boat now. I was only thinking about Skinny and I had my mind all made up, too. I didn't say anything to Westy, but on the way home I decided what I was going to do.

It was the scout trail that took me to that tenement house and if you follow a scout trail you're safe. That scout trail knew what it was doing all right. There wasn't any trail leading to the house-boat. Stick to your trail. That's the rule. And you can bet your life I was going to stick to that trail now. If that trail was going to lead to the cemetery, all right—that's what I said. But I had picked up Skinny McCord's trail and I made up my little old mind that I was going to hang on to it and follow it like a blood-hound.

That night we were going to have a special troop meeting to decide about chipping in money for our cruise up to camp, because we didn't have much left on account of spending so much for paint and lumber and different things.

I knew how the fellows and Mr. Ellsworth would be feeling about me not coming back and Westy not showing up, and I knew how the Silver Foxes would feel, especially. But anyway, I had my mind all made up. After supper my sister Ruth played a game of tennis with Westy. While they were playing I went up to my room and got out the Scout Handbook. Then I read the scout laws over, but anyway I knew them. I had read them all and I made two crosses with a pencil, one alongside of one law and one alongside another. Then I put the Handbook in my pocket and went downstairs.

It was time to go to the meeting now and so we started off.

"You seem awful funny," Westy said; "what's the matter?"

"It's patrol business," I said; "it's about—"

"Is it about me ?" he asked me.

"It's about my patrol," I said; "it's about the Silver Foxes. Did you ever hear that a Silver Fox never makes a mistake about a trail?"

"No," he said, kind of puzzled.

"You want to read up natural history," I said to him. "A silver fox knows the tracks of all the different kinds of animals and if he could talk he could tell you about them."

"Too bad he can't talk," Westy said, sort of jollying me.

"I can talk," I said. Then after a minute I laid, "It's about the Elk patrol, too."

He didn't say any more and pretty soon we got to the troop-room—that's in the Public Library. We were a little late, but I wanted it that way, so we wouldn't have any talk with anyone before the meeting started. Everyone said "hello" to us, but they were the coldest "helloes" you ever saw. "If I'd known it was going to be as cold as this. I'd have worn my sweater," I told Westy. Even my own patrol didn't say anything to us, and they all looked kind of glum. I heard Will Dawson say something about our patrol being "in bad," but I didn't pay any attention—I should worry.

Now the way we sit at the beginning of troop meetings is in three rows and each patrol is one row. The patrol leader always sits at the right hand end of the row and Mr. Ellsworth sits in front. If there are any local councilmen they sit in front with him. But it doesn't look much like that after things get started, I can tell you that, That night Mr. Bennett was there, too. He's on the Local Council.

When Westy and I went up to our row to sit down, nobody said anything to us at all, not even the fellows in our own patrol. Ralph Warner was sitting in my seat at the end, and he said, kind of cold like, "Do you want to sit down here?"

"Of course I want to sit down there," I told him; "I'm the leader of this patrol. Where should I sit?" So he moved over kind of glum and I sat down in my chair at the end, right beside the Silver Fox emblem that stands in a rack on the floor. Maybe they had an idea of electing a new patrol leader, hey? I should Worry.

As soon as we were all ready Mr. Ellsworth. called the roll and Westy and I were marked late. Then Mr. Ellsworth read a couple of notices and said the special meeting was called for several purposes. He said one was to draft a letter of gratitude to Mr. Donnelle for loaning us the boat, and one was to decide (he always says determine, but decide is easier) how much each scout could chip in for the expenses of our cruise up the Hudson to Catskill Landing.

Then he looked very serious and said one of the patrols had all signed a petition (all except two absentees, he said) asking him to order an election in that patrol for a new patrol leader.

"I have been asked," that's just what he said.

"I have been asked to administer a troop reprimand to a member of the patrol of the Silver Foxes for absenting himself throughout the day from urgent troop duties with no better excuse than a desire to play baseball. This I shall have to do. The new election is asked for in order that a patrol

71

leader may be found who will not leave his patrol and his duties on a mere pretext and not return. I authorize this election. Meanwhile Wesleigh Martin will please stand up."

I could see that Westy's face was kind of white and his lips were tight together and I knew be didn't intend to say anything.

CHAPTER XVIII. SCOUT LAW NUMBER THREE

Now, I can tell you just exactly what Mr. Ellsworth said, because I remembered it and I wrote it down right afterwards. First I was afraid Westy would say something and I didn't want him to, because — well, you'll see. So now I'll copy what Mr. Ellsworth said. Oh, jiminy, you could hear a pin drop, everyone was so quiet. He said, "Wesleigh (that's Westy, you know), I have been asked by your own patrol to give you this public reproof, and I speak for the whole troop as well, when I remind you that your action today in absenting yourself and thereby avoiding your share of the work we had undertaken to do, was unscoutlike and unworthy of you, and unworthy of the patrol whose fine traditions you were bound to guard and support. You knew that to be entitled to your share of the pleasure of this purposed cruise, you would have to do your share of the work. You knew that to — day was set apart for concerted effort by the whole troop to make this boat ready for starting next Saturday. You knew that at the urgent request of some of you boys I arranged to spend the day helping you. You were one of the boys who asked me to do this. You remember?"

"We meet here to-night after a hard day's work, pleasant as work always is, but hard nevertheless. You will have the satisfaction of knowing that you will occupy a bunk which your companions have made ready for you, and that you did not yourself hammer so much as a single nail. Arthur Ivan Arlen and Wigley Weigand, both weary and one lame, after a frightful experience, were here and helped to make the boat safe and comfortable for you. They were loyal to the Raven Patrol. I hope you may be moved to appreciate the interest and spirit which they displayed while you were playing ball.

"When you have an opportunity, Wesleigh, I would like to have you read the scout laws again and bear in mind particularly your obligation of loyalty to your scoutmaster, which of course, means to your scout duties — your troop and your patrol. I kept my word with you to — day and you did not keep your word with me. The house-boat is ready for our cruise, and I hope that you, along with all the members of the troop will find the trip enjoyable. That is all, Wesleigh, unless you have something to say."

Oh, gee, you should have heard the silence—I don't mean heard it—but there wasn't a sound. Then Westy said, "I haven't got anything to say." And then he sat down.

I knew that it was time then for me to do what I wanted to do, but I couldn't get up because I felt all shaky. I was holding to the pole of the Silver Fox emblem that was right beside me, and, oh cracky, I felt funny. All of a sudden I heard Mr. Ellsworth say that he wouldn't say anything to Roy Blakeley because the patrol was going to have an election and then I heard Will Dawson, of my patrol, say under his breath, sort of, that there'd be only one fellow to vote for me, and I knew he meant Westy Martin. Gee, I'm glad I heard him say that because it gave me a kind of an idea what to say and it made me mad, and when you're mad you have courage—you know what I mean, you can get up and talk. Jiminy, I knew I couldn't make a speech like Mr. Ellsworth with all long words, and besides I had to be careful that it didn't seem as if I was just answering him back.

So then I grabbed tight hold of the emblem pole because, I don't know, it seemed to give me courage kind of, and it was my emblem and my patrol for a few minutes yet, anyway. But oh, didn't my hand tremble. Anyway I could see that Mr. Bennett was sort of listening and I wasn't so much scared after I got up.

This is what I said, only I didn't say it as well as it sounds here on account of being nervous, but I should worry as long as I knew I was right, hey? "I heard a fellow in my patrol say just now" that's the way I began, "that there is only one Silver Fox would vote for me because I went away and didn't come back. I know he meant Westy and he's the one fellow I'd want to vote for me, anyway, you can bet. I don't care what happens, I don't, if Westy will only vote for me. Because he's one real scout and none of the rest of you know anything about scouting alongside of him—You don't. And anyway I don't care so much if I'm not leader any more, if I could only be sure you'd elect him leader—"

"He stands a tall chance," I heard a fellow say.

"About as tall as Pee-wee," another fellow said.

He was trying to be smart.

"Maybe he'll have a tall chance, as tall as the Woolworth Building," I said; "you'd better keep still. I want to ask Mr. Ellsworth if I can say something— while I'm still Silver Fox leader, that's all."

"Surely you may, Roy," he said, kind of pleasant.

"Because there's one more thing I'm going to say for my patrol. I—I started that patrol and—"

Oh, gee, then I broke right down, not exactly crying, but you know, there was something in my throat and I just couldn't talk for a minute. "Go on, Roy," Mr. Ellsworth said, and he was awfully nice, I have to admit that.

So I said how I started that patrol and did the best I could and always told the fellows to be loyal and how disgrace spills all over just like Mr. Ellsworth himself told us.

"Anyway, Mr. Ellsworth," I said, "I can't say it as good as I'd like to, because—you know—"

"Take your time, Roy," he said.

"Anyway, you remember how you spoke about the laws." I was holding tight to the Silver Fox standard and it kind of helped me to speak, and I guess pretty soon my voice didn't shake. "I know all the laws," I said, "and I think more about them than I do about stunts and adventures and things— "

"How about baseball?" a fellow said, but I didn't pay any attention to him, and Mr. Ellsworth frowned at him.

"And only to-night I looked at them," I said, "and I made marks next to two of them." Then I fumbled in my pocket and got out the Handbook, and I reminded myself of a lawyer. Anyway I could see Mr. Bennett smile at Mr. Ellsworth. "Gee, I wouldn't say anything against the laws, that's one sure thing," I said, "because they're all dandy laws, you can bet. But maybe a fellow might not know which one to obey because he can't obey them all at once, can he?"

Mr. Ellsworth said he didn't know about that and he looked kind of surprised. I should worry, I wasn't scared now. "Suppose he's on his way to obey Law 8 and keep his word and be loyal to his troop and his scoutmaster," I said. "That's Law 8, isn't it?"

Mr. Ellsworth looked surprised and said, "yes." And Mr. Bennett was smiling with and awful funny kind of a smile.

"And suppose while he's on his way he runs plunk into another law. Goodnight! What's he going to do? Maybe you don't know which law I mean by another one. It's number 3, and I can say it without even looking at the book. Even if they elect—"

I guess Mr. Ellsworth could see my voice was I trembling, because he said, "Take your time, Roy, you have us interested."

I have to admit I was feeling bad, but anyway I said the law right off without looking at the book.

3. A SCOUT IS HELPFUL.

He must be prepared at any time to save life, help injured persons, and share the home duties. *He must do at least one good turn to somebody everyday.*

"Maybe you never noticed that the part about good turns is printed in italics. You know what italics mean—you learn that in the Second Grade. It means that that special thing IS emphasized, see?"

Mr. Ellsworth was smiling a little, but anyway he was listening and so was Mr. Bennett. Gee, I didn't see anything to smile at.

Now I have to admit that I got kind of excited and I didn't know much what I was saying.

Sometimes I had to stop on account of that lump being in my throat. But anyway, I kept on and I held on tight to my emblem — the Silver Fox emblem.

"So that's what I mean," I said, "and, this morning Westy was on his way to help on the house-boat and he met" (oh, jiminies, I guess I didn't know how I was talking now, I was so excited) "and he met Skinny McCord's mother and she told him about Skinny being sick on account of a good turn he did for me — keeping Jake Holden from going to my house — and she asked him to go up and stay with him and he didn't think any more about the house-boat, and I'm glad he didn't, and I told him that, and I'm his patrol leader yet, anyway. I tell him that, I do! And he went home and got his baseball and his catching mitt and it cost a dollar and seventy-five cents, and he took them to Skinny just so as he'd kind of forgot being sick. Westy saved up to get that mitt and I know all about it. And he stayed all day with Skinny and the doctor says, he says Skinny has got to die, but anyway Westy stayed all day with him — that's what he did. And I'm glad you fellows are going to elect a new leader if you want him to reprimand Westy, be cause you'd never get me to do it, I can tell you that!"

Oh, crinkums, there wasn't a sound. It had to stop because I was gulping and all excited, but I started again, you can bet.

"And there's only one thing more I've got to say," I told them. "I got on the trail — I mean Skinny's trail. And it took me to his house in Barrel Alley. I picked up his trail down at Little Landing and it had the scout's pathfinder sign printed in the mud. And I — I'm — I'm a scout, I am, I don't care what you say, and I followed it. And maybe, for all you know, it was put there, for me to follow-maybe. It took me to where a fellow was sick, it did, and it showed me one of my own — one of the Silver Foxes, doing a good turn to

77

pay Skinny back for the good turn he did for me. And I stayed there to help and I forgot all about the house-boat, and I'm glad I did. And I hope that whoever these fellows elect, he won't let them chip in for the cruise, but I hope he'll have them chip in to send Skinny up to the country — I don't care what the doctor says. Once a doctor said that — he said that my father — "

And that's all I had a chance to say. Gee, I couldn't tell you what happened next. All I know is, I heard my Scout Handbook go kerflop on the floor and Vic Norris of the Ravens grabbed the Silver Fox emblem right out of my hand and began waving it. All of a sudden I saw Westy and he didn't say anything only put his arm around my shoulder and he started to say something and, oh, I don't know, he just couldn't. Then I heard a fellow asking him what was the matter, because he was husky, kind of, and his eyes shiny-you know. And he said he had a cold. Oh, boy!

"He caught cold from drinking out of a damp glass," Doc Carson shouted. Honest, you couldn't hear yourself think. And Pee-wee — g — o — o — d night! Then Mr. Ellsworth held up his hand and we all quieted down.

"Before we go any further," he said, "and while our lungs are working overtime I want every member of the Raven Patrol and every member of the Elk Patrol to give three cheers for the Silver Foxes, scouts, real scouts, everyone of them, and for their leader, Roy Blakeley. After that you can hold your election."

CHAPTER XIX. THE END OF THE MEETING

Oh, boy, some excitement! "Excuse me while I blush," I said. For they were all shouting and Pee-wee was on top of the table dancing and yelling, "Hurrah for the Solid Silver Foxes! Three cheers for the Sterling Silver Foxes!" Believe me, that kid is self-starting, but he isn't self stopping.

Then I told them that I had something more to say, and they shouted it was their turn to do the saying, and believe me, they did — with something left over. At last Mr. Ellsworth got us throttled down and he told me to say what I had to say, because Mr. Bennett had a word or two for us.

So I told them my idea that I'd had in my head all the time, and you just wait and see how many adventures it led to. That's one good thing about good turns; they most always start something. Already Pee-wee was started.

I told them I thought instead of keeping Tom Slade's place open, kind of in memory of him, it would be better to put Skinny McCord in that vacant place and take him up to Temple Camp and help him to get well. Then I told them how he read the Handbook, and how he was crazy about scouting, only he was scared of the fellows because he was so poor. And then I said that findings is keepings and that Skinny belonged to the Silver Foxes, and they would make a present of him to the Elks on account of Tom Slade.

"Anyway," I said, "when Tom gets back he'll be old enough for assistant scoutmaster, so it's all right."

Then Mr. Ellsworth said, "Very good," and that Councilman Bennett had something to say. This is what he said, because Mr. Ellsworth wrote it out for me, and he remembered almost just how it was. Oh, but he's one fine man — Mr. Bennett — he's on some kind of a board and he helped build the hospital and he likes the scouts and he wishes he could shin up a tree — he said so. So this is what he said.

"My young friends, I have listened with a good deal of something or other (it's too much bother to spell it out) to our young leader of the Silver Foxes, and I must say that the Silver Foxes are solid fourteen karat gold. I am a lawyer myself and I wish to express my professional admiration of the way Leader Blakeley presented his case."

"The pleasure is mine," I said under my breath, because I just couldn't help it.

Then he said like this—he said, "If Skinny McCord wishes to cast his lot with such boys as these, he shall not find the means lacking. I will furnish his suit and such sundries as he needs. I agree with Leader Blakeley that doctors are sometimes mistaken. Let us hope it may be the case in this instance. The cruise to camp must be made; let nothing interfere with that. If some of you boys wish to go into the city in the morning you may have the pleasure of purchasing Skinny's outfit. I would suggest that the Silver Foxes do this in order that their gift may go complete to their comrades of the Elks. I think I have your scoutmaster's permission to do this."

"Sure you have!" Pee-wee shouted.

"We'll go in on the 9 A. M. train," Westy said.

"What time does the 9 A. M. train leave?", Pee-wee shouted. "Oh, but it's great!" He was half crazy.

"The nine o'clock train leave at 8.60," I told him, "and you have to get a transfer—"

"To what line?" he shouted.

"To the clothesline," I said.

"You make me sick!" he yelled, "You haven't got any what—do—you—call—it—hero—something or other—"

"That talk will have to be strained through a sieve," I said. "Don't mind him, Mr. Bennett, somebody's been feeding him meat. He goes to the movies too much. He's known as the human megaphone. All step up and listen to the Raving Raven rave—only a dime, ten cents, ladies and gentlemen!"

Even Mr. Bennett had to laugh.

"Now all we've got to have is a girl," Pee-wee shouted, "because we've got a poor lad—I mean—you know what I mean—noble poverty and a boat and heroes doing good turns—"

"And Ravens turning somersaults," I said.

"And all that," he kept up, "and Roy foiled his prosecuters—I mean persecuters—"

"You mean executers," Doc said.

"And all we need now is a heroine," Pee-wee said, while he danced up and down. "A poor girl—I mean a maiden—with gold hair—if we could only rescue one—oh, wouldn't it be great."

"Even if her hair was only gold-filled it would be something," Connie Bennett said.

"You're crazy!", Pee-wee shouted, "it shows none of you know anything about stories."

Oh, jiminy, I can't tell all the stuff we shouted. You see, it was just because we were feeling so good. And Mr. Ellsworth didn't try to stop us. The next chapter is about two dollars. I don't mean it's worth that much. I don't know what I'll name it yet.

Olive oil*—that's the French way to say, "So long." Anyway, it's something like that. I should worry.

81

CHAPTER XX. MOSTLY ABOUT SKINNY

This chapter I am going to fill with some stuff about a two dollar bill.

That isn't so bad for poetry, is it? I got that idea out of a story by Sir Walter Scott—putting poetry at the top of the chapters. Mr. Ellsworth says sometimes a fellow might get killed for writing poetry. I should worry—a scout is brave.

You can bet that if Pee-wee had his way we'd have all gone into the city that very night and broken into a store to get Skinny's outfit. But nix on that hurry up business when it comes to Mr. Ellsworth. "Scouts are not made in a day," he said to Pee-wee, "and the outfit doesn't make the scout anyway, remember that."

"Any more than a merry-go-round makes a good turn," I said.

So Mr. Ellsworth went to see Skinny and his mother, and then he went to see the doctor, and he found out that Skinny wasn't going to die right then, but that something was the matter with his lungs, and that he'd keep getting sick all the time probably and wouldn't grow up. Oh, boy, when Mr. Ellsworth once gets on your trail, good night! That's just the way he hauled Tom Slade into the troop, head over heels. And look at Connie Bennett, too. Mr. Ellsworth had to hypnotize Connie's mother and now Connie's a first class scout. After two or three nights he brought Skinny to meeting, and oh, cracky, but that kid looked bad. He just sat and watched us do our stunts and he was scared when anybody spoke to him, except Mr. Ellsworth. And he was coughing a lot, too.

After the meeting Westy and I and Mr. Ellsworth took him home, and just when we left him he asked us if maybe he'd live long enough to get the pathfinder's badge. And oh, gee, it made me feel good the way Mr. Ellsworth answered him.

He said, "Well, I can't exactly promise that because I don't know how long it will take you to win that badge, but if you think you can win it inside of forty or fifty years, I think you'll be there to grab it when it comes." Oh, jingoes, but we've got one dandy scoutmaster. I don't care what you say, he's the best one in America. And when he said that, Skinny kind of smiled and then you could see how thin he was, because the wrinkles came all around his mouth.

Well, on Saturday Westy and Dorry Benton and Ralph Warner (they're all in my patrol) went into the city to get Skinny's outfit, so we could give him a surprise at the meeting on Monday night. I didn't go because I wanted Westy to have the say, and I didn't want him to think I was butting in, because Skinny belonged to him, as you might say. Besides I had to cut the grass to my sisters could play tennis with Johnny Wade — honest, that fellow is there all the time. He's got a machine, but I never saw it. I guess maybe it's a sewing machine, hey?

Now I didn't know how much money Mr. Bennett gave Mr. Ellsworth. All I know is that when the fellows came back they had everything for Skinny, or most everything. Because they came up to Camp Solitaire (that's the tent I have on our lawn) and we opened the whole business. Pee-wee was there and the first thing we knew he Was shouting that there wasn't any beltaxe.

"We used all the money we had," Westy said "and it isn't worth while asking Mr. Bennett for any more, even if there's one or two things missing."

Oh, jiminy, Pee-wee went up in the air. "Why didn't you get a belt-axe," he shouted; "don't you know a belt-axe is the most important thing of all? It's the sign of the scout! It's more important than the uniform."

"He'd look nice going down Main Street with a belt-axe and no uniform," I said; "you're crazy on the subject of belt-axes. What's the matter, are you afraid Hindenberg is going to invade Bridgeboro? You should worry about a belt-axe. Wait till he's a tenderfoot."

"That shows how much you know about scouting," he yelled; "the belt-axe is the emblem of the woods."

"The which?', Westy said.

"The emblem of the woods," he hollered at the top of his voice. "You have to have a belt-axe first of all. It's more important than the Handbook. It means woodcraft and — and — and all that sort of stuff!"

Well, first I just laughed at him and jollied him along, because I know how crazy he is about things like that — he'd wear every badge in the Hand. book on his chest if he had the chance. And he's always getting new suits and things, because his father is rich. Pee-wee's all right only he's daffy about all the scout stuff that you see in the pictures and he always has his belt-axe dragging on his belt, even when he's home, as if he expected to chop down all the telegraph poles on Main Street.

"You have belt-axes on the brain," Westy told him.

"He's got them on the belt anyway," I said.

"You ask Mr. Ellsworth about it and see what he says," Ralph Warner said. "He'll tell you it's better for Skinny to wait till he can earn a little money and then buy a belt-axe. There's time enough."

"Sure he would," I said, because I know just how Mr. Ellsworth feels about things like that. And for all I know, maybe he didn't want Skinny to have everything at the start, just so as he would be able to get some things all by himself later. Because Mr. Ellsworth thinks that's the best way. Of course, we always jollied Pee-wee about his belt-axe and about wearing his scout-knife and his drinking cup hanging from his belt right home in Bridgeboro, as if he was in South Africa, and Mr. Ellsworth always said he was the typical scout — that's the word he used — typical.

But now I began to think maybe it would cause some trouble and I hoped he wouldn't be giving Skinny any of that kind of talk. But he did just the same, and it made a lot of trouble. Pee-wee's all right, but I don't care if he knows what I said, because it's true.

On Monday we had it fixed for Skinny to come up to Camp Solitaire, and Westy and I would teach him some stuff out of the Handbook. Then we were going to give him the new stuff so he could put it on, because we wanted him to feel good — you know what I mean — when he went to meeting. We didn't want him to feel different from the other fellows. But usually we don't do that until a fellow takes the oath first.

Oh, boy, but wasn't he proud when we put the khaki suit on him, and fixed the hat on his head. He smiled in that funny way he had that always made me feel kind of bad, because it made his face look all thin. And he was awful bashful and scared, but anyway, he was proud, I could see that.

So then I opened the Handbook to page 59, where there's a picture of a scout standing straight, making the full salute, and I told him he should stand straight and try to look just like that. He said, "I ain't fat enough," but I told him not to mind, but just to look at that picture and he'd know how he looked as a boy scout.

"How soon will I be one?" he said. And I told him pretty soon.

Now I thought about that picture early in the morning and I made up my mind I would show it to him when he got dressed up. You can bet he didn't look very much like it but a lot I cared about that, as long as it made him feel good. So early in the morning before he came, I took my two dollar bill (that's my allowance my father always gives me Monday morning) and put it in the Handbook at page 59, so that I could find the place all right.

After I showed the picture to Skinny I shut the Handbook because I wouldn't need it any more and I laid the two dollar bill down on the table in a hurry, because I wanted to straighten Skinny's belt and fix his collar right and make him look as good as I could. Anyway I laid an oar-lock on the bill so it wouldn't blow away. I've got two nickel-plated oar-locks that my patrol gave me on troop birthday, and I keep them in my tent except when I go to camp.

Westy was telling Skinny how fine he looked and, oh, gee, Skinny was happy, you could see that. Of course, he didn't look very good, I have to admit it, but he had a smile a mile long.

"You're all right," I told him, "all you have to do is to stand up straight and think about scouting and the oath and the laws, and then you'll look like one."

Then he said, "I have to have one of those axes, don't I?"

"You should worry about an axe," I said! "You didn't see one in the picture did you?"

"Wasn't it because the boy in the picture was facing me, and you wear the axe in back, don't you?"

"Don't you worry," I told him, "I know that fellow in the picture and he hasn't got one on."

"One of your scout fellows says you have to have one," he said, kind of timid.

"Good night!" I said to Westy, "Pee-wee's been at it."

"He knows, too," Skinny said.

"You mean that little fellow?" I said. "Has he been talking to you?"

"Yes," he said.

"Forget it," I told him! "If that kid had his picture taken he'd stand with his back to the camera so as to show his belt-axe. If he had the Gold Cross he'd pin it on the end of his nose so everybody'd see it. The principal thing to wear is the scout smile, you take it from me. When you see Mr. Ellsworth to-night you ask him about the belt-axe and go by what he says. That's the one to go to—your scoutmaster."

"But anyway it's in the book about the axe," he said, and oh, gee, I could see how he fell for that axe. I don't know, it was something about it, I supposen "It's all right for a tree to fall for an axe, but don't you," I said. That was a joke.

"You got to have one when you go chopping trees, haven't you?" he asked me.

"You forget it," I said, and I decided I'd give Pee-wee a good bawling out after the meeting. Then I started straightening Skinny's suit and telling him how swell he looked and how he must always take off his hat to ladies. He was interested all right, but I could see how the belt-axe kind of had him, and I suppose it was because it was bright and shiny and a weapon, sort of. That's the way it is with lots of fellows when they start being scouts.

We tried to get him to go in the house to supper with us and then go to the meeting, but he was kind of scared and wouldn't. I guess it was because I live in a big house and because my father is rich—but anyway, he never acts that way, that's one sure thing. And, gee, nobody can say Ruth and Marjorie wouldn't have been nice to him too. So we left him in the tent and told him to read the Handbook, but to be sure to go home and get his supper in time to be at the meeting that evening. We made him the full salute just for fun, and oh, didn't he smile and look proud. I bet he was proud going up Main Street too.

"I'd like to get my hands on that kid," I said to Westy, as we went across the lawn; "he makes me sick with his heroes and his noble rags and his belt-axes. He's got that poor kid's brain full of fancy stuff before he's even a scout."

"That's just like him," Westy said, "but he'll get over it."

"Emblem of the woods!" I said. "Did you hear that?"

"I guess he told Skinny we were going to chop down some saplings to-morrow for stanchions on the boat," Westy said.

"Goodness knows what he didn't tell him." I said, "Skinny will be chopping down all the fence rails in Barrel Alley if Pee-wee has his way."

Oh, boy, we had huckleberry pie for supper, and didn't Westy and I have two helpings!

"There's only one thing scouts like about huckleberry pie," my father said, "and that's the taste of it."

CHAPTER XXI. SOMETHING MISSING

After supper Westy and I started for troop meeting. It was getting dark fast and we went scout-pace down the hill, because after all that had happened you bet we didn't want to be late. No, siree.

All the while we were talking about just what I ought to say when I presented Skinny to the Elks, because that's what we were going to do that night. And I was the one to do it, because I was patrol leader. Westy had a blue ribbon, because that's the Elks' color, and he was going to pin it on Skinny with an express tag that he got that day. He had it all written nice and neat on the tag.

From the Silver Foxes to the Elks.

Handle with Care.

I told him to put prepaid on it, too, and then he said it would be a good idea to put some thrift stamps on Skinny's face. Jiminy, that fellow Westy has some crazy ideas.

"Believe me, it'll be great," he said.

"The Elks will have some training to do, that's one thing," I said.

"He'll learn soon enough, all right," Westy answered.

"I guess it would be a good stunt to have a flag sticking up out of his collar," I said; "he won't mind, he'll just smile. He doesn't get mad, that's one good thing about him."

"I like to see that smile, don't you?" Westy said, "it's kind of bashful like."

"He's going to pan out all right," I said, "you take it from me."

Then we said how it might be good to put him in a barrel and mark it "A gift from Barrel Alley," but we decided not to because it might make him feel so kind of bashful and scared—you know what I mean.

All the while I knew what I was going to say, and this was it:

Scouts of the Elk Patrol, we present you with this testimonial (my sister said that was a good word to use) of our steam—I mean esteem. You get fifty green trading stamps besides. This youth is positively guaranteed to grow, if kept in the sun and to win the pathfinder's badge before the summer is out. He is made of fast colors and will not run—except when he's tracking. He should be kept away from explosives such as Pee-wee Harris.

With love and kisses from the Silver Foxes.

"Oh, it will be great!" Westy said, "we'll do it before Mr, Ellsworth takes up the collection for the cruise, hey?"

"G—o—o—d night!" I said and I stopped short.

"What's the matter ?" Westy said.

"I'm glad you said that," I told him; "I forgot my two bucks."

"I'll go back," Westy said; "you wait here." There wasn't any time to stop him and anyway, he can beat me running, I have to admit that.

"Where did you leave it?" he called back.

"I laid it right on the table," I shouted, "and I laid an oar-lock on it to keep it from blowing away. Feel around and you'll get It. Hurry up."

I saw him going back up the hill for all he was worth and then I sat down beside the road to wait for him. I got to thinking about the house-boat and the fun we'd have cruising up the Hudson and how Skinny would get fat and eat a lot, and especially how he'd stare when he saw Jeb Rushmore. He's our camp manager, and just wait till you see him, that's all I say.

But mostly I was thinking about the fun we'd have presenting Skinny to the Elks, and, oh, boy, I could just see Mr. Ellsworth laugh with that funny laugh he has—trying not to. And you can bet I was glad we had Skinny started. Because when a fellow once gets on the trail, he's a goner. Oh, bibbie, that was going to be some meeting! Pretty soon Westy came running back down the hill.

"Did you get it?" I asked him, but, of course, I knew he did. He was so much out of breath that he couldn't answer and even after he stopped he had to pant it out, kind of.

"It wasn't there," he said.

"Wasn't there!" I said; "you're crazy. Sure it was there. Where did you look?"

"I looked just where you said," Westy panted, "and all around besides. First, I felt all around with my hand and I lifted the oar-lock and it wasn't underneath it."

"Maybe you got the wrong oar-lock," I said, all excited; "there are two of them."

"The other one was hanging up," he said; "I found your flashlight on the duffel-bag and poked the light all around and I saw the other oar-lock hanging up. I threw the light on the ground, too, because there's a pretty strong breeze up there."

"How could the breeze blow it away when it was under the oar-lock?" I said. "It was a new two dollar bill."

"Well, it wasn't there, anyway," he said.

Then for a minute we both stood there and neither one of us said anything. I know what I was thinking, but I didn't want to say it. I guess Westy was thinking the same thing, too. We both sat down beside the road and after a couple of minutes, he said, "Maybe a tramp took it, hey?"

"Jerry wouldn't let anyone on the grounds," I said. Jerry's our gardener. "And besides Don wouldn't, either." He's our dog — he's a collie. "Well, it isn't there, anyway,"

Westy said; "I lifted the oar-lock and felt underneath and I laid it down again, right where it was — on a book or something. When I flashed the light it wasn't there. Come on, we'll be late. I'd let you have two bucks if I had that much extra, but I've only got two myself. You can chip in yours to-morrow, it'll be all right."

I got up and I felt awful funny.

"Anyway, there's no use being late,'" he sald, because I kind of just couldn't start.

"It isn't that I'm thinking about," I told him, "It's—"

"I know," he said, "I thought about that, too, but we've got to hustle."

So we started down the hill and neither of us said anything. Of course, we were both thinking about Skinny, but neither one of us would say it.

"Pee-wee's to blame in a way," Westy said, after a while; it's the belt-axe the poor kid was thinking about."

"No, he isn't to blame, either," I said; "he didn't mean anything—he didn't mean for Skinny to do anything like that."

"He should have kept his mouth shut," Westy said.

"Anyway," I said, "I'm not going to make that speech; I just can't. I'm not going to say anything to Skinny about it. Maybe I'll tell Mr. Ellsworth sometime—I don't know. But anyway, I can't present him to the Elks that way, I can't. I just can't. Poor kid, I don't suppose he ever saw as much as two dollars before."

"You shouldn't have left it out like that," Westy said.

After that I guess neither of us said anything. Gee, I can't tell you how I felt. I know if a fellow is low down and fires stones and calls names and all like that, even still he can get to be a scout.

But if he steals-jiminy, I've got no use for a fellow that steals. A plaguy lot I care about two bucks, but, oh, boy, I was looking forward to that meeting and how we were going to have Skinny all decorated and present him to the Elks. And now we couldn't do it, Honest, I didn't even want to see him, I didn't feel sore at him, but I didn't want to see him. Because he'd spoiled all the fun for me, that's all.

CHAPTER XXII. SHOWS YOU WHERE I DO THE TALKING

Westy said we shouldn't say anything to Mr. Ellsworth, but wait until Skinny had taken the oath and knew all the laws and all about scouting, and then maybe say something to him, how we thought maybe he had made a mistake sometime and would like to fix it right. Westy said we'd call it just getting off the trail. Westy's a mighty nice fellow, you bet, and he's a good scout. But anyway, it knocked all the fun out of that meeting for us, and I don't know what the other fellows thought.

Skinny was there in his new suit and he showed how proud he was to have it. He was always smiling in that bashful kind of a way, as if he was kind of scared but happy at the same time. Mr. Ellsworth told him to sit with us and he came over and sat in an extra chair right next to me. I guess he kind of liked to be near me—anyway, it seemed like that. I was nice to him all right, but I don't know, it didn't seem like it did before. But no fellow could get mad at him—he looked so poor, and his suit didn't fit him very good and he looked all strange and nervous.

Pretty soon I said to him, kind of half interested, you know, I said, "That's where you're going to sit, in that vacant chair where the Elks are. They're a good patrol, the Elks, and the fellow who used to sit there with them was Tom Slade. You have to try to be a good scout just like he was."

"I know all the laws, everyone," he said in a whisper.

"Do you know law one?" I asked him.

"Yup, it's the best of the lot," he said; "it teaches you about honor. Do you know the two things about scouts I like best?" he asked me.

"No, I don't," I said.

"It's that first law and the belt-axe that they wear."

"Never you mind about the belt-axe," I said.

"Yes, but you want me to tell you honest, don't you?" he blurted out. And he looked straight at me and his eyes were all kind of hollow and excited like. Gee, he was a queer kid. "You can make fun of me all you want," he said, "I don't care. Will I be a scout to-night?" "Not to-night," I told him, "we're going to turn you over to the Elks to-night. And then they'll teach you things and get you ready."

Pretty soon it came time to present him, but I didn't feel like making any fun about it. Gee! I don't know what my patrol thought about me. But anyway, Westy knew. So I just said how we found Alfred McCord and how he wanted to be a scout and we thought it was a good idea to give him to the Elk Patrol, to fill the place of Tom Slade. Cracky, there wasn't any pep to it at all.

Then afterwards Mr. Ellsworth took up the collection of one dollar and seventy cents from each fellow, to buy the eats and pay the expenses of the cruise. I had to say that I wasn't ready with it, and I guess he was surprised, because I never miss a chipping in, but anyway, I said I'd have it next day. I should worry about that.

On the way out I met Pee-wee shouting away like a machine gun. "Come on up the street with me," I said; "I want to tell you something."

When we were about a block off I said, "You listen here, kiddo. I don't want you to be shouting about belt-axes and jack-knives and things like that in front of Skinny McCord. I'm telling you that and I want you to remember it. And I've got good reasons, too. Scouts aren't made out of belt-axes and jack-knives and badges. They're made out of ideas, as you might say. You just remember what I tell you and don't be springing this stuff about the emblem of the woods and all that. A belt-axe costs two dollars—haven't you got sense enough to know that. And do you know how much it costs to take the scout oath? Not one blooming cent!"

Jiminy crinkums, he just listened and didn't say a single word. For two blocks he didn't say a word.

It was the biggest stunt he ever did.

CHAPTER XXIII. IN THE WOODS

Now I have to go backward — that's one good thing about this story, it has a reverse gear; you can go backward.

The first night we had the house-boat, Mr. Ellsworth went to see Mr. Darren, who is superintendent of Northside Woods (that's owned by the Northside estate) and he asked Mr. Darren if we could chop down some saplings to use on the boat. Because we wanted to make some stanchions for the awning, and another flagpole, and some bumper sticks. He thought that was a good idea, because lumber costs so much. Connie said the reason it was high is because they're building tall houses. So Mr. Darren marked some saplings with chalk and said we could take those.

The next afternoon after that last meeting, we all hiked over to Northside Woods to chop down the saplings. You have to go across the bridge to get to Northside Woods and then you go up the road toward Little Valley.

Westy didn't go with the rest of us because he wanted to get a book out of the library, for he thought the library might be closed when we got back.

"Have a heart," I said, "and don't be late whatever you do, because there's been enough of that kind of thing in our patrol lately."

"I'll be Johnny — on — the — spot, don't you fear," he said. And I knew he would, only he's one of those fellows that's always trying to do too much. He isn't late much, I'll say that for him, but he always comes running in at the last minute.

"Well, don't get us in Dutch," I told him, "that's all I care about."

We had a Dandy hike over to the woods. My patrol got there first and pretty soon the Ravens came along and Doc Carson had his First Aid kit — you'd think somebody was going to fight a duel, honest. "Why don't you start a base hospital and be done with it?", I said.

Pretty soon the Elks came along and Skinny was with them. As soon as I looked at him I felt kind of bad like, for I saw I was right about the two dollars. I knew I was right all the time, but now I saw it and jingoes, it spoiled all my fun. Because he had a belt-axe on and I could see he was very proud of it. He came up to me and smiled that funny kind of a smile he had, and he said, "I got one; see, I got one."

It was a new one all right, but not a regular scout-axe, and I guessed he must have bought it in the hardware store. It was what they call a camp axe—just the same only different. His belt was loose anyway, on account of him being so thin, but the axe dragged it way down and made him look awful funny, but he had on the scout smile and that's the principal thing.

"It's a good one, ain't it?" he asked me.

"It's all right," I said, but I just couldn't take it and look at it.

"It'll cut, too," he said; "and I'm going to chop down a lot of trees. And it's my very own, isn't it?"

Jiminy, I didn't know how to answer that, so I didn't say anything, only I told him not to chop down many because he wasn't strong yet. And I told him not to chop any that didn't have chalk marks. I told him to ask Connie Bennett, and to stay near him, because Connie is the Elks' leader ever since Tom Slade went away. "You do what Connie tells you", I said.

Well, the way that kid started you'd think he was going to chop the North Pole in half. "He'd be able to chop through the equator in a couple of hours at that rate," I told Connie. But anyway, he was getting fresh air and a whole lot of fun. Some of the fellows chopped and some of them cut off the branches and tied the saplings together, three or four each, because we were going to haul them as far as the bridge and then float them down to the landing.

Every little while I looked at Skinny and he was chopping away at one sapling for dear life. He had it all full of nicks and every nick had a place all to itself.

"That isn't chopping, it's what you call woodcarving," Dorry Benton said.

95

"He's a good butcher, anyway," Artie said.

Every time Skinny hit, he hit in a different place and he would never get the sapling down, I saw that, but he was having the time of his life, just the same.

"Some Daniel Boone," Will Dawson said. But I told them not to make fun of him.

All the while I kept wondering if Skinny really thought that axe was his very own like he said. And it seemed sort of funny that he could be getting so much fun out of it. Oftentimes he would get tired and begin to cough and Connie would make him sit down and rest. Then he would show his axe to the fellows and match it to theirs and say he liked his best. I don't know, maybe there was something wrong about Skinny. Maybe he was more crazy about weapons than he was about scouting. He didn't seem to think ahoot anything except cutting down that sapling, and the more of a botch he made out of it, the harder he worked. I remembered something Mr. Ellsworth said to Tom Slade about not caring more for his gun than he did for his country. But, gee, when I thought about what Skinny said about the two things he liked most, the axe and the law about honor, good night, I couldn't understand him at all.

Pretty soon I began worrying about Westy, because something is always delaying that fellow, and I even hoped that he wouldn't stumble over any more good turns, until this day's work was over. If Westy fell out of a ten-story building, he'd do a good turn on the way down — that's the way he is.

Well, pretty soon I heard him coming through the woods on the dead run. We all stopped working and laughed, because he was coming along like a marathon runner. All except Skinny-he went right on chopping away and the sapling looked as if a cow had been chewing it.

I don't know, but something or other made me feel kind of mad at him all of a sudden, and I didn't laugh at him.

96

Then he called over to me and he said, "Look how I'm chopping it down with my axe! See?" "Who's axe?" I said, because I just couldn't help it.

"Look! See?" he shouted, all excited; "ain't I a good chopper — ain't I?"

Maybe you won't understand how it was, because, gee, I can't tell things so you'll see them just right. Anyway, I'm not excusing myself, that's one thing. But I just looked over at Skinny and I said:

"I don't want to look at your axe! Shut up you little — " I was going to call him a little thief, but I'm mighty glad I didn't. "Can't you see I'm looking at something else?" I said, kind of mad. "You'd be better off if you never thought about the axe; you're a — "

Just then I heard somebody yell, "Look out, Westy, the boards are gone! You'll have to climb!"

After that, everything seemed to be all jumbled up. I saw Skinny standing near his sapling just staring at me and he looked as if I had just hit him and he didn't understand at all. He didn't even notice all the other fellows who were running. Then I looked and I didn't see Westy, but all the fellows were heading for the ditch and I knew right away what had happened. Somebody hollered, "Get your kit, Doc, and hurry up."

There was a ditch near where the saplings grew and usually there were a couple of boards across it. But they weren't there when all of us fellows went across and we had to go down into the ditch and climb up the other side. I guess the woodsmen had taken them, maybe.

Anyway, when Westy came along the path he was running so hard he didn't notice in time that the boards weren't there, and he went head over heels into the ditch. I guess I was the last one to get there, and all the fellows were standing around and Doc was kneeling over Westy, and feeling his pulse. Westy's face was all white and there was blood coming down from his eye and he looked straight up and didn't notice anybody. All the fellows were quiet and scared, kind of, and waiting for Doc to speak. But he wasn't excited, only he said we'd better get a doctor. "It isn't a fracture," he said; "it's only a cut, but anyway, we'd better get the doctor."

Then I saw some blood on the front of Westy's khaki shirt. But Doc saw it first and he said, "Open his shirt, maybe he has something hanging from his neck that cut him. Feel and see if he has a knife in his breast pocket. Open his shirt first. Give me the iodine and some bandage, one of you fellows."

I thought I ought to be the one to open his shirt, because he was in my patrol and besides we were special friends, as you might say. So I pushed through past the others and just as I was kneeling down I saw Skinny standing up on the edge of the ditch and his eyes looked big and he was all trembling and excited. There were big red spots on his cheeks and I knew that was the consumption that showed whenever he got excited. He was all by himself up there and he looked kind of wild — I can't exactly tell you..

Then I opened Westy's shirt and I saw he had a ring with two keys hanging there and they must have pressed into his chest and cut him. It kind of scared me, because there was so much blood, but Doc said, "Give me the iodine — that's nothing."

And I knew he knew what he was talking about.

While he was putting iodine in the cut I felt in Westy's pocket like Doc told me to do, but there wasn't any knife there. But there was something else there and I pulled it out. Oh, gee, I hate to tell you about it. It was my two dollar bill. I could tell because it was new and because it had a stain on it in the shape of a half circle.

I always kept oil on those oar-locks, so they wouldn't get rusty.

CHAPTER XXIV. TREASURE ISLAND

Nobody noticed me, I guess, and I just scrambled up the ditch and went away behind a tree and looked at the two dollar bill again. I guess you sure know the shape of an oar-lock all right—kind of round, but open at the top. And that was just the shape of the stain on the bill. I could have laid one of my oar-locks right on that bill and covered up the stain.

Maybe you think I was glad to get the bill back but I wasn't. What did I care about that bill? Gee, a two dollar bill isn't anything, compared to a friend, it isn't. I could have another bill right away if I wanted it, and anyway, I'd be sure to get one on Monday. It was Westy I was thinking about, because you know how you heard me say we were special friends, sort of, Jiminy Christopher! I didn't care about anything now.

Even once when I lost my bronze medal I didn't feel so bad. Then I said I guessed Westy just put it in his pocket to fool me and that he was going to give it to me. But cracky, there's no use trying to kid yourself. Then, all of a sudden I thought how he wanted me to hurry and run and how he didn't want to stop and talk much about it.

Jiminy, I didn't know what to do and I just felt like going home and going up to my room and locking the door. I knew if I ever told anybody it would be either Ruth or Marjorie. It's funny how when a fellow really has a lot of trouble he'd rather tell a girl than anybody else. You can laugh at girls, but that's true. Maybe they can't run and all that, but they kind of know all about it when you have a lot of trouble. Maybe I'd tell them, tool because they'd wonder if Westy didn't come to the house any more.

Anyway, I was glad it was me to find the two dollars and none of the other fellows. I decided that as long as it wasn't any good to me I'd put it back in his pocket if I could get a chance. Then maybe it would be kind of like a memorandum to him and he'd come and give it back when he had plenty of money sometime, maybe.

But when I went back there wasn't any chance to do that, because all the fellows were still crowding around. I stood up on the edge of the ditch and I heard somebody say that El Sawyer had gone to Bridgeboro. Doc looked up at me and he said, "It isn't bad, kiddo, don't worry." And I knew he was right and it made me feel good.

Anyway, I don't know why he called me kiddo sometimes. Because I'm leader of the Silver Fox patrol, why should he call me kiddo. But I guess he felt sorry for me, as you might say.

It was funny, but as soon as I knew Westy was going to get better, I didn't want to stay there. I was afraid he might look at me and see that everything wasn't all right. I was afraid he might see something in my eyes—you know. So I walked away, and besides, anyway, I wanted to think and I just felt I wanted to be alone by myself.

Just as I was going away one of the fellows said, "Here you go, kiddo," and chucked a book up at me. "You take care of it; it was in his pocket," he said. I guessed it was the book Westy had got out of the library and I was pretty glad because when you're all alone and haven't got any friends and everybody goes back on you, kind of, it's dandy to read a book. Because, anyway, books never go back on you, that's one sure thing, and they don't take—anyway they're good friends. When I looked at this one, I saw it was "Treasure Island" and I was glad because I always liked that one.

That fellow, Jim Hawkins, he was a fine fellow anyway. Gee, I said to myself, I'd like to have him for a friend, that's sure. Because a fellow in a book can be a friend to you just like a real one. Even better, sometimes.

CHAPTER XXV. THE SHORT CUT

One thing, I hoped they'd all go home soon so I could sit down on a log and read some more in that book. Only lately I read it, but cracky, that doesn't make any difference when it's a good book. I thought I'd go back to the ditch pretty soon—as soon as Ed Sawyer came with the doctor. But anyway, I wanted to be alone now.

So I stuffed the book in my pocket and strolled over to where we had been cutting the saplings. Then I went over close and looked at the one Skinny had been chopping. I guess I didn't know what I was doing and thinking about. Anyway, now that I looked at it, I was sorry I made fun of him and got mad at him. It wasn't only because I knew he didn't take the two dollars, but anyway, I felt sorry for him.

I couldn't see him anywhere around and he wasn't in the ditch, I knew that If he had been there then, you bet I'd have been all right with him. It made me feel bad when I looked at that sapling an hacked and standing up just as strong as ever. He must have chopped away on it for half an hour and about all the poor little kid did was to get the bark off. Right close by, I saw his belt axe lying just where he left it. It had Skinny marked on it, and I guess he did it himself. It made me feel kind of sorry for him that he called himself Skinny. It was his axe, anyway. And I felt like kicking myself. And I saw how he had been trying to be a scout just like the other fellows, poor little kid. It wasn't any of my business where he got the money. It was his, anyway.

Then I began kicking the chips around with my foot and saying, "Poor kid." And I said I guessed he'd die before he could ever chop down a tree. Because, now since I had seen those red spots on his cheeks I knew how bad he was. I knew he didn't have any strength at all, and all the time something he had said kept running in my mind. "I like the one about honor." "Poor little Skinny," I said. I was feeling bad, anyway.

An of a sudden I heard a sound and saw three or four fellows scrambling up out of the ditch. So I went over there and just as I got there, I saw something that I'll never forget, you can bet.

First I thought it was a ghost, and all the fellows were flabbergasted. It was Skinny standing right near and clutching hold of a tree, and he was all trembling and I thought he was going to fall down. Honest, I never saw anything like the way he looked. His hair was all flying loose and it made him look wild, because it wasn't cut. And his eyes were all like as if they were on fire.

"I got him," he said, "I got him—he's coming. He's getting—out of—out of his automobile. I got him because I'm—I'm a swamp-rat!" Thats just the way he said it, and he hung onto the tree and his fingers were all thin like an old man's and the spots were in his cheeks. "He's coming!" he panted out.

Just then I could see Doctor Winters coming through the trees with a little black bag. He must have left his machine out on the road about a hundred yards away. And I guess Skinny must have jumped out and run in ahead to show him the way and he just kept saying, "I got him, I got him! Because I'm a swamp—rat—everybody says so—and I know the short cut—now can I have a badge—maybe—sometime? Maybe am I a scout now?",

I just looked at him and it gave me the creeps, because I knew what he had done. And I remembered now how people called him a dirty swamp-rat. Many a time I'd heard them call him that. Just a dirty little swamp-rat. And now, he was sort of proud of it.

First, I couldn't move and I just couldn't speak. Then I went up to him and I said—I didn't care for the doctor or anybody—I said, "Skinny, there's one fellow here who knows what the marshes are and that's me. Because I came near getting swallowed up by them."

"It's—it's—short-cut," he just panted out. "All I want to tell you is," I said, "there's not another scout in the whole troop could do it—do you hear! You're not a swamp-rat, you're a swamp-scout," I said.

Then I was going to say more, only Skinny seemed as if he was going to fall and the doctor kind of seemed to want me to move away. Anyway, I went over and got Skinny's belt-axe to carry it home for him.

CHAPTER XXVI. IN MY OWN CAMP

As soon as the fellows knew for sure that there was nothing much the matter with Westy, they scrambled out of the ditch and all stood around Skinny, praising him up and he was so excited that he didn't talk straight, but sort of yelled at them. The only ones with Westy were the real doctor and Doc Carson, and Doc was helping him fix the bandages better.

When I saw them down there it made me feel as if I'd like to go down and say something to Westy. His face was all white and the bandage on his head made him look—oh, I don't know—sort of as if he might die. And then I'd be sorry I hadn't said something to him. Because I had known Westy an awful long time.

So I went down and pretty soon the doctor went up to see Skinny and Doc Carson went too. So I was alone with him down there, but his eyes were shut on account of his being weak from losing so much blood, and he didn't notice me.

Anyway, I slipped that two dollars into his shirt pocket because I didn't want it anyway, and I thought maybe it would be a memorandum to him, like I said. Besides I didn't have a right to keep money I got out of another fellow's pocket.

I said, "It's me, Westy; the reason I didn't come around was because all the other fellows were here. But now you're alone I want to tell you that I'm glad you're not hurt bad."

He just looked at me and he said, "I went—I did it."

First I didn't know what to say, and then I said, "Never you mind, I guess you were kind of crazy. We all get crazy sometimes. I was crazy when I thought Tom Slade was lying once. Never you mind."

"I guess I was crazy," he just said, and then he shut his eyes and I didn't bother him any more—only just sat there. I don't know what made him tell me, but anyway, I was glad.

Pretty soon I helped him to Dr. Winters' automobile because he limped pretty bad. Skinny went in the automobile, too, and Doc Carson, but they didn't ask me. All the fellows went along the road, too, because nobody felt like hauling the saplings that day, and I didn't, that's sure. I said I was going back to get Skinny's axe, and I was glad when I was all alone in the woods. That's the best place to be if you've got any troubles and you want to think.

And I kind of didn't want to think about Westy, so I thought about Skinny just to keep everything else out of my head. Because I knew it wouldn't ever be just the same again with Westy and I didn't want to think about it. In the troop it would be all right, and maybe in the patrol too, but it wouldn't ever be just the same again with Westy and me.

I was glad that I'd be interested in Skinny and now I could see he was different from all of us kind of wonderful-I don't know how to tell you. His eyes were so big, and wild, and starey. And he said things in such a funny way and he got so excited. Up at Temple Camp, afterwards, Mr. Ellsworth told Jeb Rushmore that Skinny was inspired, but I don't know just what he meant. An I knew is we were even scared of him sometimes. He never called any of us by our names — that was funny.

Pretty soon I went home. It was all dark in the woods and dandy for thinking, and I was glad I had one friend, anyway, and that was Jim Hawkins in the book. I guessed maybe that was the reason that Westy got the book, because only lately I had read it, and I had told him so much about it. All the way home I kept thinking about Westy and I wished I had never found that out.

Mostly at night I sit on the porch with my mother and father, but that night I went to my tent and lit the lantern and sat there. I like a lantern because it reminds you of camping. Nix on electric lights up at Temple Camp, that's what Jeb Rushmore says. Gee, he has no use for electric lights — electric lights and umbrellas. But, anyway, I've got a wire from our garage to Camp

Solitaire (that's my tent) and a bulb for when I want to read. Jerry says I ought to pay for tapping the garage current. I should worry.

I sat down and began reading 'Treasure Island' all over again. I skipped a lot because I had only just lately read it, and pretty soon I was reading about in the middle of it, where they start off in the ship. That's the part I like best. All of a sudden I couldn't see the reading very good and I noticed there was a stain on the page.

Here's where I wish that I knew all about writing books like a regular grown up author, because I have to explain something to you and, cracky, I wish you could see that book, because then it would be easier. First, I didn't think anything about it at all, only I noticed that the stain was on the left hand page. Then, all of a sudden I noticed something about that stain that got me all excited. It was in the shape of a ring, kind of.

Right away I knew what it meant. I picked up one of my oar-locks and laid it on the stain and it just covered it. So I saw I had damaged the book when I had it before. That's one thing you're not supposed to do — damage books out of the library. If you keep a book till its overdue, that isn't so bad, because then you just pay a fine. Connie says that's being a good bookkeeper.

But to damage a book — g — o — o — d night!

CHAPTER XXVII. THE GENTLE BREEZE

I was just thinking how funny it was that Westy got this very same book that I had, but maybe it wasn't so funny, because that was what put it into his head to get it—seeing it in my tent. Anyway, I was glad it came back to me, because now I saw what I had done and I made up my mind that I'd buy a new book for the library.

Then I was thinking how I'd have to tell Westy about it, and, oh, I don't know, I just didn't know how to go and speak to him. I wasn't mad at him, but anyway, I felt as if I didn't want to see him—yet. Anyway, I didn't have any money yet and books like that cost a lot.

All of a sudden I heard Don start barking and then he stopped. So I knew somebody was coming that he knew. Then I heard somebody say, "You're always suspicious, ain't you," and oh, I felt awful funny, because I knew it was Westy. It seemed as if he might be saying that to me, but I knew he was saying it to Don—just kind of jollying him. Maybe you think you can't jolly a dog but you can. You can Don, anyway.

I didn't know what I would say to him, because I thought probably he'd come to give me my two dollars and say he was sorry and must have been crazy or in a hurry. Jiminy, any excuse would be good enough for me, as long as he told me straight out about it, like he did in the ditch. And maybe things would get to be all right after a while. But I couldn't understand how he could come up the lawn whistling and jollying Don and feeling so good. I don't mean because he was hurt, because I knew that wasn't so bad, but I didn't set how he could be feeling so happy.

Pretty soon he came in and Don was jumping up all around him and wagging his tail. "I'm glad you're well enough to come out," I said.

"You should worry about me," he said; "I just have to limp a little, that's all. I'm a swell looking Silver Fox, hey?" And then he gave me a push and rumpled my hair all up and said, "You won't be ashamed of me on account of my honorable wounds, will you? I was a punk scout to go and do that."

Gee, I didn't know what to think, because it wasn't anything to be laughing at, that's sure.

"Do what?" I said.

"Run right into that ditch."

"Is that what you meant you did—when you told me?" I said, kind of disappointed.

"Sure it is," he said, "I'm a swell scout, hey? Going headlong into a ditch!"

I just listened to him and I felt pretty bad, because now I saw that was what he meant.

Then he gave me another shove and he said all happy like, "But I'm the champion boy sleuth all right. Look at this—here's your two bucks and Skinny never took it at all"?

"I—I know he didn't," I said.

"How did you know," he shot right at me.

"Because," I started to say and then he rumpled my hair up some more and began talking and never gave me a chance.

"Because it was right in that copy of Treasure Island that's laying there," he shouted, "and I'm one big gump, that's what I am! I got that copy of Treasure Island out of the library this morning, because you were telling me about it, and right there in the middle of it was your plaguy old two buckarinos!"

Just for a minute I looked at him and I knew it was just like he said, because he was laughing—he was so blamed happy about it.

Oh, boy, didn't I feel good!

"How in the dickens did it get there?" he said.

"That's one puzzle," I answered him.

"Anyway, you've got your two bucks back."

"A lot I care about that," I said; "jiminy, I've got something better than two dollars, and that's friends, you can bet."

Then I showed him the stain on the page of the book and we both sat there gaping at it and thinking.

"I'm hanged if I know," Westy said; "it would take Tom Slade to dope that out."

"Maybe Skinny was looking at the book and shut it with the two dollar bill inside," I said.

"How about the stain?" Westy asked me.

"Jingoes, it's a puzzle," I said.

All of a sudden he laid the book down open and laid the bill on it and then he laid the oar-lock on the bill. Then he just sat there like as if he was studying. Pretty soon he said, "We have to get a new copy for the library, anyway. Do you mind if I make another stain on this one? I've got a sort of an idea."

"Go ahead," I said.

So now I'll tell you just what he did and you'll see how it solved the puzzle. And, believe me, you'll have to admit that Westy's a pretty smart fellow. If you have an old book you don't care anything about, you can even try it and you don't even need an oar-lock. Westy turned to a new place in the book and then he laid the bill down on the right hand page. Then he laid the oar-lock on the bill. "That's just exactly what you did when you laid the bill down in such a hurry that night you were fixing Skinny up. You laid it on the open book just like that—see?"

"Maybe I did." I said, "but what's the big idea, kind sir?"

"Well, then," he said, "I came up here to get your two bucks for you, didn't I? And you remember I told you there was a breeze blowing? Now what did I do—in the dark?"

"Search me," I said.

"Why, you big galook, I felt around in the dark and lifted the oar-lock off the bill and then felt there for it, but the breeze was too quick for me. It blew the page over and I slapped my hand down on—what?"

"Another page," I said; "good night!"

"Good-bye two dollar bill," he said, "it was between those two other pages. That's why there was a stain on the right page in the book. There was a stain on the bill made by the oar-lock and when the page and the bill blew over, the fresh oil on the bill kind of stamped itself on the left hand page. You didn't damage the book. You only damaged the bill. It was the breeze that damaged the book—see?"

"Believe me! I'll be responsible," I told him.

"That breeze was a thief," he said.

"It'll come to grief some day," I told him. Then we both began to laugh.

"And it's lucky I got that book out of the library," he said. "There was your two bucks tucked away all nice and neat between the pages. It was just where Jim Hawkins was starting awake on the ship."

"Narrow escape," I said, "hey? If you hadn't taken the book out just when you did, good night, the ship might have started and good-bye to my two dollars."

"You crazy Indian," he said.

"And all the time I was saying Jim Hawking was honest and a good friend and all that, and all the time he had my two bucks."

"Believe me I wouldn't trust that fellow with a postage stamp," Westy said.

Laugh! Oh, boy, I thought I'd die laughing—and Westy, too.

CHAPTER XXVIII. JOLLYING PEE-WEE

That's the reason I'll never trust a gentle breeze. In books you find all kinds of nice things about gentle breezes, but look out for them, that's what I say. Whenever I leave my bathing suit on the grass to dry, I lay a good big rock on it, you can bet. I'd trust Skinny with a hundred dollars, I would, and Westy too, but gentle breezes — Nix. They're so plaguy sly and sneaky like.

Westy and I went and bought a dandy copy of Treasure Island for the library. It cost us a quarter more than my two dollars, but we should worry.

Now I have to tell you one other thing that happened before we got started on our cruise, especially because it has a lot to do with our cruise.

The next morning we all went back to Northside Woods to tie up the saplings and drag them over to the river. Then we were going to use a rowboat and tow them down and maybe float some of them down. I told you about our old launch, but it's too shallow to use a launch up as far as Northside Woods.

All the fellows were there except Skinny, because the doctor made him stay home on account of being all played out. I bet that doctor had some scrap with him. One thing sure, Westy and I stuck together. By noontime we had all the stuff hauled over to the river and some odds and ends of kindling wood besides, to take in the house-boat. We filled the rowboat with the small stuff and towed the saplings and started downstream that way. The tide was running up and it was almost full and we had some job bucking it. Some of the fellows wanted to wait till it turned and come down with it. But I said that would be an hour maybe and that if the tide didn't want to turn and go with us, we should worry.

Now that there wasn't anything left to do, but tow the stuff down, all the fellows except Westy and I and Pee-wee started to hike it home. We said we'd take him with us in the boat so that he could bail, because that boat is built like a sieve.

"If it keeps on leaking like that," I said, "there won't be any water left in the river-it'll all be in the boat."

"It's pretty hard bucking the tide," Westy said.

"And we're going up hill besides, too," I told him; "remember that."

Well, you should have seen Pee-wee. "What are you talking about-up hill!" he shouted. "When we begin going down hill," I said, all the while winking at Westy, "she'll go easier, thank goodness."

"We'll have to put on the brakes," Westy said.

"Do you know why they talk about towing lumber?" I asked Pee-wee; "because it's measured by the foot."

"You're crazy!" he shouted.

"Just the same as when they use it for back fences, it's measured by the yard," Westy said, all sober like.

"Sure—back—yard," I said.

"You think you can jolly me, don't you?" Pee-wee shouted.

"You just keep on bailing," I said, "and don't stop. When the tide begins turning you won't have to bail so fast."

Jiminy, Pee-wee didn't know what to think—whether I was kidding him or not. "Why won't I?" he wanted to know.

"Because it will be going the other way," I said, "see? It'll be flowing away from the boat."

Oh, boy! Pee-wee just emptied the bailing can down my neck.

And that's the way it was all the way down. Cracky, but we had Pee-wee so crazy that he'd bail up a can of water out of one end of the boat and empty it in the other end.

"What's the difference whether it's inside or outside?" Westy said, "as long as it's there. I bet there's a lot of canned salmon in this river."

"Canned what? Pee-wee shouted.

"Keep on bailing," I said; "canned salmon is what he said, but I think there are more pickled herrings. There's lots of pickled herrings in the Hudson, I know that."

"You mean smoked herring," Westy said, all the while rowing and looking around very sober like at me.

Oh, boy, didn't Pee-wee open his eyes and stare! He didn't know whether to take it for a joke or not — we were so serious.

"I suppose it's on account of the smoke from the big Hudson River boats," I said, "just the same as Oyster Bay."

"What about Oyster Bay?" Pee-wee shouted.

"When the water gets all stewed up in rough weather, they get stewed oysters."

"Not always," Westy said.

"No, but most of the time," I said.

"Oh, sure," Westy said, "but I've seen lots of red lobsters that didn't come from Red Bank—"

"It's boiling makes them red; you big galook!" Pee-wee yelled.

"Oh, sure," I said, not paying any attention to him, but all the while rowing hard and looking around very sober like at Westy, "because I know there are lots of bluefish caught near Greenland and you'd think by rights they ought to be green."

"Sure," Westy said, "just the same as the fish caught in American River out west, are red, white and blue."

"And stars," I said.

"Sure the river's full of starfish and striped mackerel — stars and stripes. That's why you have to stand up in the boat if you're rowing on that river ."

"Oh, sure," Westy said, "that's why so many boats get upset."

Good night! you should have seen Pee-wee.

"Keep on bailing, kiddo," I said, "keep plenty of water in the river."

"Maybe it would be better to let a little more come into the boat," Westy said, "so as to lower the water in the river, so we can get under the bridge."

"The both of you make me tired!" Pee-wee yelled; "do you think I believe all that stuff?"

Good night, some circus! It's always that way when Westy and I get out with Pee-wee.

Pretty soon we 'heard a loud whistling and we wondered what it was, because it didn't sound like a train and it sure wasn't on a motor-boat.

Then Westy began asking what we were going to do about power after we got our stanchions and bumper-sticks and all that fixed. I said we'd have to get Jake Holden to tow us down around into the Hudson and then get somebody to tow us up. Westy said Mr. Ellsworth thought it would be cheaper to take our little three horse power engine out of our launch and install it in the houseboat.

I said, "That would be all right, only it would kick us along so slow that we'd spend all our vacation on the trip and wouldn't have any time at camp." Cracky; I didn't want to start back as soon as we got there.

"Well, then, there's only one thing to do," Westy said, "and that's for us to get towed and that costs a lot of money."

All the while the whistling kept up and it was awful loud and shrill, sort of, as if it was mad — YOU know how I mean.

"I know what it is," I said; "it's somebody waiting for the bridge to be opened."

"Good night, they stand a tall chance," Westy said.

"It's a tug, that's what it is," Pee-wee said; "I can see the smoke. It's going up in a big column."

"It's more than a column, its a whole volume," Westy said, looking around. "There must be books on that boat; the smoke is coming out in volumes."

All the while we were getting nearer to the bridge and it was easier rowing, because the tide was on the turn.

Now maybe if you fellows that read this don't live in the country where there's a river, you won't understand about tides and bridges and all that. So I'll tell you how it is, because, gee, we're used to all that, us fellows.

Jimmy Van Dorian, he lives right near the bridge in a little shanty and he's lame and he's a bridge tender. You don't get much for being a bridge tender and mostly old veterans are bridge tenders. Anyway, they don't get much out our way, because big boats don't come up and they don't have to open the bridge often.

When we got down to the bridge we saw that the tide was right up so we even had to duck our heads to get under, and right on the other side of the bridge was a tugboat standing facing upstream and its whistle was screeching and screeching just like a dog stands and barks when he's mad. It seemed awful funny because it was a small tug and it made so much noise.

"It ought to be named the Pee-wee," Westy said.

"Nobody's paying much attention to it," I told him.

Just as we came under the bridge we could see a big fat man, oh, Christopher, wasn't he fat, standing up in the pilot house pulling and pulling the whistle rope, for the bridge to open. Sometimes he'd pull it very fast, just like you do with the receiver on the telephone when you're good and mad because Central don't answer. And it was pretty near as bad as the telephone, too, because he went on tooting and tooting and tooting and nobody paid any attention to him.

CHAPTER XXIX. JIMMY, THE BRIDGE-TENDER

Pretty soon the big fat man stuck his head out of the window and he shouted, "What's the matter, is everybody deaf around here? Here, you boys, where's the bridgeman?" Honest, you'd think I had the bridgeman in my pocket. I told him I didn't know where the bridgeman was. Oh, but he looked mad. He had an awful red face and white whiskers and I guess he must have been used to ordering people around — anyway, he looked that way.

He said, "Here I am on the down tide, the water going out every minute and got to run up to North Bridgeboro yet. It's a —" he said what kind of an outrage it was, but I wouldn't tell you. Oh, he was hopping mad. "I'll get stuck hard and fast in the consarned mud," he said, "if I ain't back and past this here Sleepy Hollow in forty minutes — that's what I will!"

I hollered up to him that I'd row across to Jimmy's house and see if he was asleep.

"Asleep!" that's just the way he shouted. "Do bridgeman sleep on full tide up this way? Don't he know the harbor and waterway laws? I'll make it hot for 'im — I will." And then he began pulling the whistle faster and faster.

"Somebody must have been feeding him meat," Westy whispered to me.

"He's good and mad, that's sure," I said. Even while we rowed across to Jimmy's shanty I could hear him shouting between the whistlings and saying he'd have the bridgeman up for deserting on flood tide and putting him in the mud. And jiminy, I have to admit that he was up against it, because the tide was running down and by the time he got up to North Bridgeboro and back, it would maybe be too low in the channel. One thing, Jimmy had a right to be there, especially at flood tide, I knew that. But I guess the reason he wasn't was because nothing but little motor boats ever came up our river and they can always crawl under.

Jimmy lives all by himself on account of being old and his people are all dead. I said to Westy that maybe he was just asleep, so we knocked and knocked, but nobody came to the door. Then I knew he wasn't there at all or else maybe he was dead.

"Anyway, we'd better find out," I said, "because it's mighty funny him not being there, seeing that he never goes away anywhere."

All the time we could hear that old grouch shouting about Bridgeboro and our river and saying it was Sleepy Hollow and Dopeville, and the river was a mud hole. But it isn't and don't you believe it.

"Anyway, I'm going to climb in through the shed window," I said, "and see if maybe Jimmy is sick or dead." I could see that Pee-wee was not exactly scared but sort of anxious, and I was too, I have to admit it.

Westy and I got the shed window open, all right, because Jimmy wasn't careful about it, on account of not having anything worth stealing, I suppose. I was kind of shaky when we went into the first room, because that was where he slept and I thought maybe he'd be lying there dead.

But he wasn't there at all. Just the same we stood there looking at each other, and we were both kind of nervous, because Jimmy's clothes were lying all around on the bed and on the floor, and a chair was knocked over, and it looked just as if somebody had been rummaging in the room in a big hurry. The door into the other room was closed and, I have to admit, I didn't feel like opening it.

"I bet somebody's robbed him and killed him," Westy said, kind of low.

"That's just what I'm thinking," I said, "and when we open that door we'll see him lying on the floor dead, hey?"

"Anyway, we have to open it," he said.

"I'll open it if you don't want to," I told him.

But, anyway, neither of us opened it. We just stood there and I felt awful funny. It was all still and spooky and you could hear the clock ticking, and I counted the ticks. It sounded spooky, going tick, tick, tick.

Then Westy said, "Shall I open it?"

"Sure," I said, "we've got to sometime."

So he opened it just a little bit and then, all of a sudden, he pushed it wide open and we looked into that other room.

CHAPTER XXX. GONE

In the middle of the room was a table Jimmy always ate his meals at, and on that table was a big square piece of paper and there was a big envelope on the floor. But there wasn't any sign of Jimmy. Oh, boy, didn't I feel good on account of that. Westy read the paper out loud and it was something about a convention of the Grand Army, or something like that. It said how all the members of some post or other were asked to go to Saratoga on account of that big convention and it was addressed to "Comrade James Van Dorian." Gee, I felt awful sorry for him, sort of, because I knew how it was with him.

"He just couldn't help it," Westy said, "he got ready in a hurry and went. I guess he took all the money he had saved up-poor old Jimmy."

"He'll lose his job, that's sure," I said.

Even while we were standing there I could kind of see him getting dressed up in a hurry in that old blue coat he had, with the buttons all falling off it, and starting off with his crutch. Maybe he just got his pension money, hey?

All the while the whistle on the tug was blowing and I was afraid people would come around and maybe they'd all be on the side of the tugboat man and be mad at Uncle Jimmy.

Jiminy, I wasn't mad at him, anyway. And I could hear that old man shouting about all the things he was going to do and about the bridgeman deserting and leaving him in the mud.

"Hurry up," Westy said, "let's find the key-bar and we'll open it for him, we can do it all right."

So we looked all around in a hurry, but we couldn't find it anywhere. The key-bar is what you open the bridge with, you know. It's kind of like a crow-bar and you stick it in a certain place and walk around pushing it. It isn't so hard when you get started on account of the bridge being balanced right and it's geared up, too. But what's the use if you can't find the key-bar?

118

"It must be somewheres around," Westy said, all excited.

Oh, didn't we turn things inside out! But it wasn't any use—we couldn't find it.

"Don't let's bother," I said, "I've got an idea, come ahead—quick!" I didn't even stop to tell him what I was thinking about, but I hustled back into the boat, with Pee-wee after us, wanting to know what we found inside.

"A couple of mysteries," I panted out.

"How many?" he wanted to know.

"And a couple of ghosts thrown in," I said, "Hurry up."

On the way across I told the fellows to please let me talk to the old man, because I had something particular to say to him. I was panting and rowing so hard, that I couldn't tell the fellows then. Anyway, I guess Pee-wee had that house haunted and filled with German spies and Uncle Jimmy murdered and goodness knows what all.

We pulled up right alongside the tug-boat and I called out to the old man that I wanted to tell him something and to please let me come up. I was all trembling, but anyway, I said it right out and I didn't wait for him to say yes, because he was too busy saying other things to say it.

Westy and Pee-wee stayed in the rowboat and I went right up into the little house where the old man was. Oh, boy, wasn't everything polished all nice and shiny! Gee, it was nice up in there. The wheel looked awfully big and the compass, you could just see your face in it. And it smelled kind of oily and nice up there. Wouldn't I like to live in a place like that!

The old man was smoking a pipe and he blew out a lot of smoke—it was kind of like a barrage.

Then he said very stern and gruff, "Well, sir?"

Oh, boy, wasn't I shaky! But I started right in, and when you once get started it's easy, that's one sure thing.

I said, "Maybe you'll only be more mad when I tell you but I heard you say something about Uncle Jimmy deserting. Twice you said that. And I thought maybe you might be a veteran, hey? Maybe that's a crazy thing to think, hey?"

All he said was, "Well, sir," and he blew a lot of tobacco smoke at me and looked at me with a frown, all fierce, but I wasn't scared.

"I only kind of deduced that," I said, "and anyway I've got to admit you've got reason to be mad."

Even still, all he said was, "Well, sir," and he held his pipe so I thought maybe he was going to chuck it at me — good night!

"Anyway, if you were a soldier, maybe you'll understand, that's all. Uncle Jimmy, that's what we call him, he went away to the Grand Army Convention — that's where he went. I'm not saying he had a right to go, but one thing, big boats like yours never come up this way, so the bridge doesn't have to be opened very often — sometimes not all summer. It's kind of just bad luck for him, that's all. But, one thing sure, I know how it is to be away when I ought not to be, I do. And I'm no better than he is, that's one sure thing. I'm a boy scout," I told him, "and my scoutmaster says you have no right to make bargains about things that are wrong. But anyway, maybe you wouldn't think this would be trying to make a bargain with you and sticking up for somebody that did wrong. So I thought I'd ask you if you'll please promise not to write to the government people, and I'll promise you to open the bridge for you in ten minutes. He's lame, Uncle Jimmy is, and he got that way in some battle, and he has to use a crutch. And that's the reason they gave him a job. I see your tug is named General U. S. Grant, and maybe he was fighting with General Grant, hey? You can't tell.

"We can't find the key-bar, but about a month ago, the old key-bar fell in the river, and I know where it is. Maybe you think I'm crazy, but I'm dive and get it for you, if you'll only promise not to tell on Uncle Jimmy, because he couldn't help going. Maybe you don't understand, but he just couldn't. I've got the swimming badge and that's for diving too. All you have to do is to give me some rope, so I can take one end of it down and then you can haul it up and the key-bar will be tied to it. You can be dead sure. Because what a fellow has to do, he can do. Only you have to make me the promise first 'cause that'll help me to do it."

CHAPTER XXXI. THE CAPTAIN'S ORDERS

Maybe it wasn't a very good speech, but anyway, he was nicer than he was before and he had an awful funny twinkle in his eye.

Then he said, "So you know how to dive, huh, sonny? Can you keep your mouth shut?"

"Sure, you have to keep your mouth shut when you dive," Pee-wee yelled up from the rowboat, and then the old man just had to laugh.

"I mean when you're on land, sonny," he said.

"Sure I can," I told him.

"Well, then" he said, "if any of you scout kids goes about sayin' as how Uncle Jimmy went away to the convention, and I ever meet you in your old skiff, by the Big Dipper I'll run you down and cut you in half, that's what I'll do! Do you hear?" he shouted. "If you ever run afoul of the General Grant in the bay or anywheres else, by thunder, I'm Cap'n Savage, I am, and once upon a time I was Major Savage, and I should be at that there convention myself, instead of standing here blowing away at a better soldier than me!"

"Don't you care, we'll forgive you," Pee-wee shouted up.

"Keep him quiet, will you?" I called down to Westy.

"Ask me something easy," Westy said.

"And so you think you can dive," old Captain Savage said, "or is that just boy scout talk? Do I stand a chance of getting upstream and down again to-night, or not. Where do you say that key-bar is?"

You can bet I knew just exactly where it was. It was under the east span of the bridge and just underneath about the fifth or sixth plank from the centre. I knew it was hard bottom down there, too. So Captain Savage and the other man he had gave me a thin rope and we fastened one end on the deck. I tied the other end of it around my waist in a loose French sailor's knot, so I could pull it off without any trouble under water.

Then I dived. I had to come up a couple of times without it, but the third time I got hold of it lying on the rocks, and quick as a flash I loosened the rope from my waist and tied it onto the keybar. Then I came up, sputtering.

"Pull," I sputtered, "you've got it; only pull easy." Then I scrambled up on the deck. Believe me in less than a minute the tug-man and Westy and Pee-wee were on the bridge and had the key-bar fixed in its socket. Then we started to push and around she went—slow at first; then faster.

Oh, boy, wasn't I glad to see old General Grant march through. Just as I was going to get in the rowboat, Captain Savage stuck his head out of the window and shouted, "Here you, youngster; you come in here. We have to overhaul accounts."

"Scouts don't accept anything for a service," Westy shouted.

"I ain't a-talking to you," Captain Savage shouted; "you other feller, scramble aboard and come up here! Don't they learn you nothin' about obedience in them thar scouts—huh? you scramble up on board here like I tell you!" Oh, boy, I knew he meant me.

CHAPTER XXXII. I MAKE A DANDY FRIEND

That was the first time I ever rode in a tug-boat, and believe me, it was great. I stood right beside the wheel in that little house and pointed out the channel to Captain Savage all the way up to North Bridgeboro. That's one thing I sure know — the channel. Anyway, if you don't know it, follow the abrupt shore. But with a tug-boat, good night, you have to be careful because a tug 'draws so much water. He was going up there after a lumber barge, he said.

First, he didn't say anything, only smoked, and it was like a fog in there. Pretty soon he said: "So you youngsters don't take nuthin' fer services, huh?"

"We have to do a good turn if we see a chance," I told him.

Then he wanted to know all about the scouts, how they were divided into troops and patrols and everything, and after I told him all that, we got to talking about our vacation and about Temple Camp, and especially about the house-boat. I asked him if he thought a three horsepower engine would drive the house-boat up the Hudson, so we could get as far as Catskill Landing in a couple of weeks.

He said, "It would be more like a couple of years, I reckon."

"Good night!" I said, "if it takes us two years to get there and we have to be home inside of a month, I see our finish. I suppose it costs a lot of money to get towed."

He said, "Wall now, whin I bring in a Cunarder and back her into her stall, it stands them in a few pennies."

"You said something," I told him.

"'N I don't suppose your troop has got as much money as the Cunard Line," he said.

"Gee, we've only got about four dollars now," I told him; "I suppose we couldn't get towed as much as a mile for that, hey?"

"Wall, four dollars don't go as far as it used ter," he said; "maybe it would go a half a mile."

Then he, didn't say anything, only puffed and puffed and puffed on his pipe, and kept looking straight ahead of him, and turning the wheel ever so little. After a while he said there wasn't water enough in our river to drown a gold fish, and he didn't know why we called it a river at all. He said he couldn't imagine what the tide was thinking about to waste its time coming up such a river. He said if a bird took a drink in the river while he was upstream, it would leave him on the flats. He was awful funny, but he never smiled.

When we got up to the mill at North Bridgeboro, he got the barge and started downstream with the barge alongside. All the while he kept asking me about the scouts, and I told him about Skinny, and how we were going to take him up to Temple Camp with us, so he could get better, maybe.

Then for quite a while he didn't say anything, only puffed away and pretty soon we could see the bridge and I knew we'd have to open it again.

But anyway, I could see a lot of fellows there and I knew they were all from our troop and that they were waiting to open the bridge for General Grant.

Pretty soon Captain Savage took his pipe out of his mouth and began speaking, only he didn't notice me only kept looking straight ahead.

"You know how to port a helm?" he said.

I told him no — not on a big boat like that anyway.

Then he said, "Wall, there's lots o' things you got to learn, youngster. And there's one thing about tug cap'ns that you got to learn, see?"

I told him that was what I wanted to do — learn —

"Wall, then, I'll tell you," he said-this is just what he said — "I'll tell you, you are in a mighty ticklish place 'n I don't just see how you're going to get out of it."

For a minute I was kind of scared.

"I ain't sayin' you're not a brisk lot, you youngsters, because you are, and no denyin'. All I'm sayin' is you're in a peck of trouble — that's all."

Then he didn't say anything only looked straight ahead out of the window and kept on smoking. Gee, I felt awful funny.

Then I said if we did anything that wasn't right, cracky, we didn't mean it anyway, that was sure, and we'd do whatever he said. And I said I knew it wasn't right for us to break into Uncle Jimmy's shanty, because I couldn't think of anything else we'd done that was wrong.

Then he said, "'Tain't so much wrong, as 'tis a conflict of rules, as the feller says. Yer see, the trouble is tug-boat captains are a pretty pesky, ugly lot, as yer can see from me, and when it comes ter services, it's give or take. Now I was thinkin', that if you youngsters don't let me tow you up as far as Poughkeepsie next week, I'll just have to write and notify the authorities about Uncle Jimmy and make a complaint. I kinder don't like to do it by reason of him being an old veteran, but it's up to you youngsters. Either scratch out that rule of yours, or else see Uncle Jimmy lose his job. Take your choice, it's all the same to me."

G — o — o — d night! Jiminy, I didn't know what to say to him. I guess I just stood there staring and he looked straight ahead out of the window and smoked his pipe, as if he didn't care either way.

Pretty soon he said, "I'm going up to Poughkeepsie next Saturday with a barge, and I'll give you youngsters till Friday to decide. You can send me a line to the barge office or the Pilots' Association, or else you can leave me and old Uncle Jimmy fight it out between our two selves and Uncle Sam."

The fellows opened the bridge for General Grant to go through and Captain Savage let me out on one of the cross-beams, without even stopping. He didn't even look at the fellows as the tug went through, only looked straight ahead of him and puffed away on his pipe, as if he didn't even know that there were such things as scouts. We just stood there

126

watching the tug churning up the water, as she went faster and faster until she was gone around the bend.

"He's a kind of an old grouch," Pee-wee said.

"It's good you happened to think about how he used that word desert," Doc said.

Then Connie said he wouldn't want to be his son, and Artie said he wouldn't want to be around the house with him on a rainy Sunday, and I let them go on knocking him, until they got good and tired and then I said, "Do you know what he wants to do?"

"I bet he wants us to go and be witnesses against Uncle Jimmy," Pee-wee said; "he'll never get me to be a witness, you can bet."

"Wrong the first time, as usual," I said; "he wants to tow the house-boat up as far as Poughkeepsie for us next week."

Well, you should have seen those fellows.

"What did you tell him?" Pee-wee yelled.

"I told him that I was sorry, but that scouts couldn't accept anything for a service—not even favors."

"You're crazy!" Pee-wee shouted; "did you tell him that?"

"Sure I did," I said, very sober, "and he got so mad he's going to have old Uncle Jimmy sent to jail—just because I told him we couldn't let him tow us to Poughkeepsie."

"You make me tired!" Pee-wee screamed, "do you mean to say that if a fellow does a good turn to another—an old man—and it turns out to be a good turn on somebody else, and he says—the other one that has a boat—that he'll make a lot of trouble for the other one we did a service for—do you mean to tell me that the other one has a right to say he'll make trouble for him, and if he does we haven't got a right to let him do a good turn to us, so that the other one we did a good turn for can get under a bridge—it's a good turn to let him do us a good turn, isn't it? Let's hear you deny that?"

"You're talking in chunks," Doc said; "pick up the words you spilled and straighten 'em out."

"Hold him or he'll fall off the bridge," Artie said.

"Do you mean to tell me that we haven't got to let him pay us back so as to save Uncle Jimmy?" Pee-wee fairly screeched.

Oh, boy, you should have seen him.

"There is yet time," I said, just like an actor, sort of. I said, "There is yet time to fool him—I mean foil him. We have till Friday to accept his offer."

"Who's got a pencil?" Pee-wee shouted.

Good night! You should have seen that kid.

CHAPTER XXXIII. SO LONG-SEE YOU LATER

So that's about all I can tell you now, but pretty soon I'll tell you about our cruise up the Hudson and all about the fun we had on the house-boat and on Captain Savage's tug. Oh, boy, he turned out to be one fine man. And I'm going to tell you all about Skinny too, and about the fix we got into about that tramp that slept in the house-boat. You remember that fellow, don't you. Some scare we had, believe me.

And you'll hear about Temple Camp and Jeb Rushmore, and you'll get to know us fellows a lot better. Gee, I hope you'll like us. Mr. Ellsworth says I'm a pretty good author, only I took such a long run there wasn't any space left to jump in. I should worry. Some authors don't run at all, they only walk. Believe me, you have to drag some of them with a rope.

Anyway, we've got acquainted now and that's something. In the next story there's going to be some girls — and some snakes, too. Especially one snake. Gee, but girls hate snakes — snakes and mice. Anyway, Mr. Ellsworth told me to write just the same as I talked, so if it's no good, maybe that's the reason. You should worry. Maybe you'll like the next one better, hey?

Anyway, you'll like Temple Camp, that's one sure thing.

THE END

Milton Keynes UK
Ingram Content Group UK Ltd.
UKHW040904110923
428455UK00004B/308